An Amish Christmas in Rocky Comfort

By

Jeanie Smith Cash

An Amish Christmas in Rocky Comfort

Jeanie Smith Cash

This is a work of fiction. Names, characters, places and incidents, either are the product of the author's imagination, or are used fictitiously and any resemblance to actual persons living or dead, business establishments, or locales, are entirely coincidental.
An Amish Christmas in Rocky Comfort

Unless noted, Scripture references are from the New King James Translation. Cover Art by Jeanie Smith Cash. Publishing History First Edition 2022, Published in the United States of America

Endorsements

Jeanie Smith Cash's sweet, inspirational romance stories are like little kisses from Heaven! Readers who prefer clean, wholesome romance they wouldn't be afraid to share with their daughters and granddaughters...this is what you're looking for. Not just an "author of Christian romance," Jeanie is a "Christian author of romance. Any Christian reader knows the difference."
Delia Latham, Inspirational Romance Author

Endorsements

Jeanie Smith Cash is an experienced writer with several books published. She writes inspirational romance. Her characters seem real and she does a great job of pulling the reader into the story from the first page. I enjoy all of her books, but I especially like the Amish stories. Jeanie's stories are clean, enticing, and a pleasure to read.
Barbara Warren, Inspirational Romantic Suspense Author

Dedication

I'd like to dedicate this book to,
Robyn Rosewicz,
my Precious Sweet Christian
Daughter. The Lord Blessed us the
day she was born and I love her so
very much. She's always there for
me and she gives me
encouragement in every book I
write, and in all that I do, which I
so appreciate. I thank the Lord for
her every day. HUGS to you
Sweetheart and may God Bless
you and keep you safe always.

Acknowledgements

I'd like to thank my **Lord and Savior** for His love, for His watch care over us and for all of the blessings He gives us every day. He makes this all possible, for I wouldn't be able to write a single word without His loving guidance.

Acknowledgements

And as always, thank you
to my loving Christian
Husband, Andy,
who takes me to do research
for my stories.
He is my own special hero and my
best friend, whom
I love with all my heart.
He's always there for me no
matter what I need and I
Thank the Lord for him every day.
I'd also like to thank
My sister Chere Snider for
critiquing my stories and my
family for their love,
care, encouragement and support.
Thank you to all of my

readers that support and encourage
me by reading my books and
asking when
my next one will be available.

Amish Glossary

Aunt-Aenti
Ausbund-Amish Hymnal used in
worship service
Baby-Boppli – Bopplin
Boys - Buwes
Brother-Bruder
Budget-Amish Newspaper
Child-Kind
Cleaned Up-Redd Up
Come komm, kume
Coffee-kaffi
Crazy Ab im Kopf
Darlin - Liebling
Daughter-Dochder
Doctor -Doktor
Eck-bride and groom table
Englischer–Non Amish Person

Family – Familye
Farmhouse - Farmhaus
Father-Daed
Friend - Frienden
God-Gott
Girl-Maedel
Good-Gut
Good Morning-Guder Mariye
Good Evening-Guten Tag
Good night-Guder Nacht
Grandchildren-Grandkinner
Grandfather-Daadi
Grandfather House, attached to
back of main House-Daadi Haus
Grandmother-Mammi
Grandparents-Grosseldre
Good Morning-Guder Mariye
House-Haus
How Are You-Wie gehts
Is - ist
I Love You-Ich lieb dich
Love-Lieb
Mother, Mom - Mamm

Man-Mann
Men-Menner
My - mie
My Love - Liewi
Wedding attendants for bride and
Groom - Newhockers
Oh-Ack
Ordnung-Written and unwritten
rules of the Amish
Prayer cap-Kapp
Pretty-Schee
Quick - Schnell
Running around period that begins
at age sixteen and ends when the
young person is baptized into the
Amish Faith - Rumspringa
School-Schul
A Baptized member who leaves
the community can no longer
communicate with the Amish until
they return, confess and ask
forgiveness in front of the
congregation – Shunned

School - Schul
Sister-Schweschder
Son-Sohn
Sweetheart, Dearest – Liebling or
leibchen
The - der
Thank you-Danke
Uncle-Onkel
Usher - forgher
Wife-Fraa
Wonderful-Wunderbaar
Yes-Jah
Your welcome-Welkom

Scriptures

Bear with each other and forgive whatever grievances you may have against one another. Forgive as the Lord forgave you. Colossians 3:13

For God so loved the world that He gave His only begotten Son, that whoever believes in Him should not perish but have everlasting life. John 3:16

If you confess with your mouth the Lord Jesus Christ and believe in your heart that God raised Him from the dead, you will be saved. Romans 10:9

Jesus said, I am the way the truth and the life. No one comes to the Father except through Me. John 14:6

Chapter One

Levi Graber climbed out from under the covers in the one room apartment where he'd slept in a single bed for the last year. He had left his Amish community of Rocky Comfort, MO on Rumspringa and this was the best he could afford on the money he'd saved and brought with him. He was homesick and missing Emily Mast. She was the girl he'd *liebed* all of his life and questioned his sanity now, in making the decision to leave her to go out on *Rumspringa*. Had she waited for him? Please *Gott* I pray she did. It was time to go home. He wasn't happy in the *Englischer's* world. He should never have left. It had been the biggest mistake he'd ever made. He'd been working for a company building furniture. He decided he might as well go home and work for *daadi* and *d*aed at Graber and *Sohns* Furniture, he would be much happier doing the same job at home with his *familye*. Once the decision was made he had packed what few things he had, in his duffel bag last night and was ready to go to bed.

The next morning, he took a quick shower, looked around to be sure he hadn't missed anything, grabbed his duffel bag and headed on foot to the bus station. His bus left at 2am. He wanted to be home in time for breakfast. The weather would soon be turning cold, but it was just the end of October so it would be nice for a couple more weeks.

Three hours later he arrived at the bus station in Springfield, Mo. He had called Enterprise car rental yesterday so when he got off of the bus they had a car waiting and he would drop it off in Monett, Mo. This was the last time he would be able to drive or use his cell phone. He wouldn't be allowed to do either one, once he arrived back home to his Amish community and was baptized.

He noticed the leaves were turning on the trees. He remembered right before he left last year, he and Emmy had enjoyed seeing the changing of color in the trees. Emmy commented on how beautiful they were as they turned orange and yellow for fall. Thinking of Emmy wrenched his heart. Why had he been foolish enough to leave her? He prayed she hadn't found someone else. He *liebed* her and wanted to eventually make her his *fraa,* if she'd still have him.

Once he arrived in Monett, he turned the rental car in and called a driver that his family used, to come get him and give him a ride home to his community. He should be home in time to share the breakfast meal with his family and he prayed his *daed* would allow him to stay. Just the thought of his *mamm's* cooking made his mouth water, he was starving.

Levi grabbed his duffel bag and headed out to meet the driver as he saw him pull up in front of the rental car building. He opened the front door and slid in next to Bob, as he dropped his bag over the seat to land in the back floor board." *Danki* for *kuming* to get me, Bob."

"Sure thing, Levi. How are ya? It's good to see you. It's been awhile."

I'm doing well, *danke*. I am home to stay. I should never have left and I am anxious to get home.

About a half hour later Bob dropped Levi off in front of his parent's *farmhaus*. Levi paid and thanked him before he left. Levi stood at the end of the driveway and looked around. This was the home where he was raised and he hadn't realized until now just how much he had missed it, his family and Emmy. As he walked up to the door he prayed his family would welcome him back and that Emmy would forgive him for being so foolish. Just as he was about to step up onto the back porch, his *daed* walked out of the barn. He headed toward the *haus* with Levi's *bruders*, Joshua, Jacob, David, Mark and Luke right behind him. His *daed* stopped as he looked up and realized Levi was standing by the porch. His *daed* began to run toward him and Levi met him half way.

"Levi, *mie sohn*." His *daed* wrapped Levi in a hug, then

stepped back and looked at him. "Are you well, *mie sohn* and are you home to stay?"His green eyes so like his *sohns* glossy with unshed tears.

Levi didn't realize until that moment just how much his leaving had impacted his *familye*. Sadness at what he had put them through gripped his insides and he vowed right then he'd never do something so selfish again." I am *gut, Daed* and I am home to stay if you will allow it."

"This is your home, *sohn*, of course you can stay, we have missed you and are glad to have you home. Let us go inside, your *mamm* and *schweschders* will be pleased and relieved to see you are home, as well."

His *bruders* patted him on the shoulder and Jacob the oldest of the twins, said, "We are glad you are home too, Levi," and all the *buwes* nodded in agreement as they went inside.

"Karen, Look who is here." Gideon said.

Levi's *mamm* looked up from the stove where she was preparing breakfast with his sch*weschders* Deborah and Maryann. "*Ack mie sohn!*" *Mamm* cried hugging him. After a minute she pulled back and said, "Let me look at you. Are you all right? Are you home to stay?"

"*Jah,* I am okay and I am here to stay. I have missed all of you and I am so glad to be home."

"We are glad you are home also," his *schweschder's* said at the same time and then laughed.

Levi, laughed with them. "I am glad to be home as well."

"Sohn, you can place your bag in the mud room and then let us sit and have this meal your *mamm* and *schweschders* have prepared for us." Gideon said and pulled the chair out at the head of the table and sat down along with the *buwes.* It felt so *gut* to be sitting in his place at the table once again with his *familye.*

Mamm and the *maedels* placed the food on the table and then joined them. They all bowed their heads and *daed* said a silent blessing over the meal. When he was finished he started the dishes of food around the table

"Have you seen Emily? How is she doing?" Levi asked as he accepted the first dish and dread filled his heart at the look that *mamm* and the *maedels* exchanged. "What is it, is she all right?"

Mamm looked over at him, "Emily doesn't participate in anything except Sunday church services. She doesn't even stay for the meal afterwards. Her *mamm* told me at the last quilting bee, that Emily does her chores at the *haus* and then spends the rest of her time in her room."

"What? Emily loves quilting bee's and meals after service."

"*Jah*, she always did, Levi, until you left. Nancy said she does not go or do anything away from the *haus* except church service." Deborah told him.

Levi closed his eyes for a moment. *Gott, please forgive me for the damage I have done. Please help me to be able to fix this.*"This is *mie* fault. I have to go see her and try to repair the damage I have done." As soon as the meal was over, Levi picked up his empty plate and placed it in the sink. '*Danke* for the delicious meal *mamm* and *maedels*. *Daed*, is there anything you need me to do before I go to try to see Emily and can I use your buggy?"

"*Nee*, you go ahead and you can help feed and milk tonight. Your horse and buggy are in the barn."

"*Danke, Daed*. I appreciate you and the *buwes* taking care of Leo while I was gone. I will be here to help this evening for sure and certain." Levi kissed his *mamm's* cheek before he left to head to Emmy's *haus*.

Chapter Two

Emily Mast sat on her bed. She had just finished helping her *mamm* and *schweschders* with breakfast and to *redd* up of the kitchen. She glanced out the window at the beautiful trees in the yard. She *liebed* the change of colors in the fall. Although it made her sad this year as she remembered enjoying the change of colors last year with Levi Graber. She didn't understand his need to go on *Rumspringa*. She had thought they would be baptized and then get married after completing their baptismal classes last year. When he had *kume* to her *haus* after the last class and told her he had to go on *Rumspringa*, before he could go through the baptismal service, she couldn't believe it. He told her he *liebed* her, but he would never be truly happy until he had a chance to experience *Rumspringa*. She was devastated, nothing seemed to have any meaning for her since the day he had left. She had decided when he said he'd be back in a year, that she *liebed* him so much, she'd wait for him to return. He'd been gone for a year today, so she decided he must not be *kuming* back after all. Her heart was breaking at the thought of going on without him. She had hope until this morning, thinking he would return and they could still be together, but that obviously wasn't going to happen. Tears ran down her cheeks and she didn't even have the desire to wipe them away, her heart was breaking. *Please Gott help me through this, I thought he would kume home. She cried.*

******

Levi pulled into the driveway in front of the Mast *haus*. He prayed Emmy's *mamm* and *daed* would allow him to see her. He stepped down as, Noah, Emmy's *Daed* came out onto the porch.

"Levi?" Noah's eyes widened in shock.

The expression on his face didn't surprise Levi, after all he had been gone a year, so Noah Mast wasn't expecting to see Levi in his driveway. "*Jah*, Noah it's me. I am back. I plan to stay and be baptized into the church. The *Englicher's* world is not for me. This is *mie* home, for sure and certain. Leaving here was a mistake I don't plan to ever repeat."

"That is *gut* to hear. I am glad you are back to stay and I am sure your *familye* is too."

"*Jah*, they were very glad to see me and to know that I am home to stay." He smiled. "Is Emily home?"

"*Jah*, she is in her room."

'Could I possibly talk to her?" He asked hopefully.

"Are you sincere about taking the baptism and staying here in the community."

"*Jah* Sir, I am. I will never leave again. This is *mie* home. It was a big mistake to ever leave in the first place. I have regretted it many times since I left. It was the biggest mistake I have ever made and I do not plan to repeat it ever."

Noah looked at him for a few minutes before he said anything else and Levi just knew he was going to turn him away.

"She hasn't been seeing visitors, so I do not know if she will see you, but I will go ask her. Sit here on the porch swing and I will be back."

Levi sighed in relief. *Danki*

Noah."

"Do not say *danke* yet, I cannot promise she will see you," He said as he went inside.

Levi sat on the swing and prayed Emmy would see him. He glanced up when he heard the door open. It was Faith, Emmy's *mamm*.

"It is *gut* to see you back home where you belong, Levi. I am sure your *mamm* and *daed* are very happy to have you here to stay. I have brought you a cup of *kaffi* and a cinnamon roll."

"*Danke,* I appreciate it. They are *mie* favorite." He smiled.

"*Jah*, I remember." She smiled back just as Emmy hesitantly stepped out onto the porch.

"Levi, you are home to stay?" She looked at him and asked reluctantly, because he figured she was afraid of the answer.

"*Jah*, I am. I told you I would be back in a year and it's been a year today."

"She stood looking at him, as her *mamm* quietly slipped back into the *haus*. But Emmy didn't say anything or make a move to sit down. His heart nearly sunk at the hurt that was clearly visible on her face. "Emmy, would you please sit here beside me so we can talk?" He waited for what seemed like an eternity, but was actually only a few minutes before she sat on the swing next to him. *Danke, Gott at least that is a first step. Please help me to be able to convince her to see how sorry I am and how much I lieb her.*

Danke, I appreciate you sitting with me. I am so sorry. I never meant to hurt you. *Ich lieb dich* with all *mie* heart. I was so foolish to ever leave you and I pray you can forgive me." Levi waited anxiously. For her to say something.

"You broke *mie* heart, Levi. " A tear slid down her cheek.

The sight of that tear nearly crushed him, realizing the pain he had put her through. "I am so sorry, Emmy. I never meant to hurt you. If you can possibly forgive me and give me another chance. I promise I will never do anything to hurt you again and I will never leave you. I have realized what a mistake I made and I will not make that choice a second time. I will try *mie* very best to make it up to you."

"I am not sure I can trust you anymore, Levi. I never thought you would leave me last year. I thought we had something special, a true *lieb*."

"I am so sorry. We do have a true *lieb* and it is special, Emmy." She didn't respond, she just sat there and the sadness on her face as she looked out across the yard, crushed him knowing this was his fault. "Emmy, I am so sorry for hurting you. I made the worst decision and the biggest mistake of *mie* life, when I left you a year ago. I pray you can forgive me *Leibchen* and give me another chance. I *lieb* you so very much."

Chapter Three

Emily *liebed* Levi so much her heart was breaking. This was what she had been praying for, that Levi would *kume* home. Could she trust what he was telling her? She had been so miserable since he left. She did not want to be alone any longer, but could she trust him not to break her heart again, if she gave him another chance? *Gott, what should I do?* She glanced at

Levi. He was so handsome with his crystal green eyes so unusual, she had never seen anyone with that color eyes except him, his *daed* and siblings. His hair the color of honey, was cut shorter than it was when he left. Just the sound of him calling her Emmy, warmed her heart. She had thought she would never hear him call her by his special name for her again. She closed her eyes for a moment to try to get her emotions under control. She did have to admit to herself that he did keep one of his promises. He had *kume* back in a year, as he said he would. "Can I trust you. Levi? You broke *mie* heart and devastated *mie* world when you left, I will not survive it if you leave me again?" She looked directly at him waiting for his answer.

"I will never leave you or hurt you again, Emmy. You have *mie* promise on that. If you will give me a chance I will show you, I will do everything I can to make you happy."

She waited just another moment, then looked over at him, before she said, "I will give you another chance, Levi, but we need to take it slow."

"We can do that, Emmy. I will give you all the time you need. *Ich lieb dich, Liebchen.*"

"*Ich lieb dich* too, Levi."

"Can you *kume* for supper tomorrow evening?" His heart was singing, he *liebed* her so much.

"*Jah*, I would like that." She smiled.

Just seeing her smile warmed his heart. "*Gut, danke.* I will *kume* for you a little after 5pm if that is okay."

"*Jah*, I will be ready."

Levi stood and said," I will see you tomorrow evening then. *Danke*, Emmy. You will not be sorry, I promise." He smiled and went out to his *buggy* and climbed in. He waved as he backed out and started down the road to his parent's *farmhaus*. Everything was right in his world once again for the first time in a year. *Danke, Gott.*

Levi pulled into the barn and unhitched Leo his horse. He rubbed him down and gave him some water and oats before heading into the *haus*.

Levi walked up behind his *mamm* and kissed her cheek. With a big smile he said, "Something smells *gut*." He told her.

"I take it all went well with your visit to Emily." She smiled back at him.

"*Jah*, it did she is *kuming* tomorrow *nacht* for supper." He grinned.

"That is *gut* for both of you. She has been very unhappy since you left, it will be *gut* to see her smile once again. *Sohn*, do not break her heart again." His *mamm* told him firmly.

"Do not worry*, Mamm*. I will never hurt her again. I *lieb* her so much, it broke *mie* heart to see her so sad.

Mamm looked at him for a moment before she said, Supper is almost ready. Go wash up, your *daed* and *bruders* just came in and they went out to wash up too and will be back soon. *Sohn*, I am so glad you are home."

"*Danke, Mamm*. I am glad to be home and I am starving. I will be right back."

"That is nothing unusual, you were always hungry." She smiled as he went out to the mud room to wash for an early supper.

After *daed* said the silent prayer, he started the food around the table. "Levi, we are having a barn raising this Saturday at Abraham and Abigail Masts place. You need to join us there, we need everyone to help rebuild their barn." Gideon said as he passed Karen the platter of bacon.

"I will be there *Daed*. What happened to the Mast's barn?"

"Lightening hit it and it caught on fire, we were able to save all of the animals, equipment and most of the hay before it burned.

"I am glad for that at least.'

Levi knew that was Emmy's grandparents barn.

"We will all be there, *Daed.*" Jacob said and Joshua, his twin agreed.

"*Jah* and we will be helping by serving food and drinks all day." Deborah told Levi and smiled. It is *gut* to have you home, *bruder.*

"*Jah*, it is." All his siblings agreed at once and they all laughed.

"*Danke*, it is *gut* to be home too." He grinned.

"*Daed*, the north fence needs to be repaired." Jacob said," I noticed when I brought the horses in this evening, it had a bad place that's not going to hold if something spooks one of them. If you can get the fencing when you go to town tomorrow, I can fix it in the afternoon. I have the day off at the store since I am helping *Daadi* fix his barn door in the morning. As soon as we are done I can *kume* home and fix the fence."

"Jacob, I can help you with the fence. I am not picking Emmy up until 5 o'clock." Levi offered.

"*Danki, bruder*. I would appreciate that." Jacob grinned.

"That is *gut buwes*. I will pick up what you need, when I go to town in the morning for supplies." Gideon told them.

Chapter Four

The next morning after showering and getting dressed, Emily went downstairs to help with breakfast. She couldn't believe she was actually going to be with Levi and his *familye* to share their evening meal tonight.

Brenda and Susan were helping *Mamm* when Emily walked into the kitchen. "I'm sorry, I overslept. I will *redd up* the kitchen after breakfast." She hugged her *mamm* and younger *schweschders*.

"You were tired but you are here now. Please set the table and by that time the *menner* will be here ready for their meal." *Mamm* went back to the stove to get the *kaffi*.

Where is Nancy? Emily asked as she heard *Daed* and her *bruders* coming in the door just as she finished setting the table.

"She left early, *Mammi* asked your *schweschder* to open the Bakery this morning, so she could go to the store to pick up some supplies."

Emily helped *Mamm* and her

schweschders set the food on the table, by the time they had it ready the *menner* were sitting down. *Dead* said a silent prayer over the meal. When he was finished, he cleared his throat to let everyone know he was through and started the food around.

"The barn raising at *daed* and *mamm's* place is tomorrow morning." *Daed* sat his *kaffi* on the table and glanced at *Mamm"*

"That is *gut*. I know they will be glad to have it done," *Mamm* said and continued to eat her breakfast.

"It is so sad that *daadi* and *mammi* lost their barn, I feel so bad for them." Emily looked first at her *daed* and then her *mamm*.

"*Jah* it is, but the two weeks have passed quickly. *Danke, Gott*. I am so glad that after the

lightening hit their barn and
caught it on fire, that the structure
was the only thing that was lost.
No one was injured and we got all
of the horses out safely, it could
have been so much worse. I am so
glad *Gott* was watching over all of
us. Our *frienden* and neighbor's
are *kuming* together tomorrow to
rebuild it for them, so they will
have a new one by evening." *Daed*
told them and then finished his
breakfast.

"*Jah*, that is *gut* and that no
one was injured. I will help
Nancy, Brenda, Susan and *Mamm,*
with the food and serving it."

That will be *gut, danke
dochder.*" *Mamm* smiled as they
went to the sink to *redd* up the
kitchen, as her *Daed* and *bruders*
went out to the barn.

Once they had the kitchen

finished, Emily said, "I'm going to go, I need to be at the bakery in a half hour to help *Mammi.* She said last *nacht* when I went to see if she needed help, that I could have Sarah's part time job, since she quit to get married. *Mammi* said she would be happy for me to *kume* to work. She told me they have several orders going out today and she needs all of our help to accomplish them. I'll be home in time to help you with supper though, before Levi *kumes* to pick me up."

"That is *gut, Dochder,* I am so glad to see you going out and participating in the community once again, but your *schweschders* can help me, you go with Levi and enjoy your evening." She smiled.

"Danke, Mamm." Emily returned her smile and headed out

the kitchen door.

When Emily walked out to the barn, Steven already had Ruby, her horse, hitched to her buggy and helped her up onto the seat.

"*Danke*, little *bruder,* I appreciate this."

"He laughed. Little? I'm a foot taller than you." He grinned.

"*Jah*, but you will always be *mie* little *bruder*." She grinned back.

"Emily, I'm glad you are happy again. I did not like seeing you so sad," Steven said.

"*Danke*, Steven. I am glad to be too." Emily backed Ruby out onto the road and headed toward town. A few minutes later she pulled her buggy into *Mammi's* barn behind her shop and unhitched Ruby. Emily walked into *Mammi's* Bakery about ten minutes later and her best friend Rebekah Yoder, greeted her with a big hug.

"Emily, I can't believe you are here. I have not seen you out except at church in so long. Are you all right? "

"I'm okay. I went over to *mammi's* last night and asked her if she needed some help since Sarah's last day was yesterday and she hired me. We'll have lunch soon and we can catch up. She grinned. "

"That will be *gut*." Rebekah grinned back. I will look forward to it. I was just going back to ask Abigail what she wanted me to start on this morning. She and Nancy are in her office. *Kume,* we can walk to the back together. I'm really glad to see you out. I've missed you."

Emily followed Rebekah back to the office where they found *Mammi* and Nancy unpacking supplies and logging it in a book,. *Mammi* glanced up and Emily grinned.

"Emily," *Mammi's* face lit up with a bright smile. "She rounded her desk to wrap Emily in her arms. I am so glad you decided to *kume* to work with us."

"*Jah*, I am glad I did too and it's *wunderbaar* to be here. When you said last night you could use me part time I was grateful.

"I am so glad to see you out of the *haus*."

"I am glad too and Monday, Wednesday and Friday, from seven to three, will work out well for me, *danke.*" *Emily* smiled.

"*Welkom.* We have missed

you. You can start helping Nancy and Rebecca unload these boxes of supplies."

"*Jah*, I can do that." Emily was glad to have something to occupy her until it was time to go supper with Levi and his *familye*.

"*Wunderbaar.*" *Mammi* reached into a drawer behind her and handed Emily an apron. That will keep the dust from the boxes off of your clothes."

"*Danki.*" Emily took the apron and tied it around her. After unloading all of the boxes, Emily left Nancy stocking the supplies. She walked up next to Rebekah at the front counter, to see if she needed some help and Emily started frosting half of the cupcakes Rebekah had been working on.

Chapter Five

"Levi came to see me yesterday."

Rebekah stopped and looked at Emily. Surprise clearly showed her face. "Levi is back?"

"*Jah*, he got back yesterday morning and came over to see me. He asked me to have supper with him and his *familye* tonight."

"Be careful, Emily. He nearly destroyed you when he left."

"I know, but he apologized and told me had made a terrible mistake by leaving. He asked for my forgiveness and said that he never meant to hurt me, he said he *liebed* me and he was home to stay. He said if I would give him another chance he would never do anything to hurt me again and that he would spend the rest of his life making me happy. I *lieb* him Rebekah, I feel I have to at least give him a chance."

Rebekah looked at Emily for a moment before she said, "I know you do and you will never know unless you give him that chance. Just be careful and I will pray it will work out between you two."

"Danki, Rebekah, you are the

best friend I could ever ask for."
Emily hugged her.

"That goes both ways.'"
Rebekah hugged her back.

By the end of the day, Emily
was more than ready to go home.

"Thank goodness it's 4:30. It's
been quite busy today." *Mammi*
turned the closed sign and pulled
the curtains together on the door.

"Thank you *maedels*, for all of
your help today. Emily, we are
glad you are back and that you
will be working part time helping
us. It would have been a chore to
get all those boxes unpacked and
the cupcakes frosted without you.
I will see you both on Saturday at
the barn raising. It will be so nice
for *daadi* to have a new barn for
the horses, our two cows and the
cats." She smiled.

"*Jah*, it will and we will be

there to help." Emily said and hugged her *maami.*"

"*Jah*, we will be there also to help. I cannot imagine how hard it has been this last two weeks without a barn."

"*Danke, maedels*. It has been, but, *danke Gott*, the weather has been pretty *gut*."

Emily and Rebekah agreed as they walked out the door and to their buggies together. Nancy had left after lunch. She only worked on Saturdays and on the days when *Mammi* had an order coming in, that needed to be stocked.

"Emily, untied the lead rope and ran her hand down Ruby's smooth neck.

"I will see you tomorrow at *maami and daadi's*, Rebekah. Be careful going home."

"*Jah*, and you be careful too. I

will be praying everything goes well tonight with Levi."Rebekah grinned and stepped up into her buggy. I better be going." She waved as she pulled away.

Emily waved back as they both pulled out of the small barn *Mammi* had for their horses. When Emily pulled into the driveway and up to the barn, Steven met her.

"I'll take care of Ruby, so you can go inside and get ready to go to supper, Levi should be here soon."

"*Danki*, Steven." Emily smiled as he helped her down from the buggy. At fifteen, her little *bruder* already towered over her.

Emily ran upstairs after asking *mamm* if she could help her, but *mamm* said *nee* to go ahead and get ready to go with Levi. Emily changed to a Sunday dress and re-combed her hair, before changing her apron and *kapp*. She ran downstairs and Emily heard *mamm* greet Levi. She invited him in, just as Emily stepped off of the bottom stair.

******

Levi smiled at Emily and she smiled back.

"Are you ready to go?" Levi asked.

"*Jah*," She smiled

Levi took her coat from Faith, and helped Emmy into it.

"Be careful, it is supposed to rain after while." Noah told Levi.

"I will be careful and I will bring Emily back home safely." Levi promised as they walked out the door. Levi walked Emily over to the buggy, helped her up onto the seat and covered her legs with a quilt, before he went around to step into the driver's side. Are you warm enough?" He asked as he backed the buggy out onto the road and headed to his *haus*.

"*Jah,* I am fine. *Danke.*" She smiled at him.

Being close to her made his world right once again. Danke Gott, that she waited for me. Please help me to be able to make her happy.

As they backed out onto the road and started toward his *haus* he said, "I have an appointment to see Bishop Yoder tomorrow right after the barn raising, while you *maedels redd* up. I want to see if I can be baptized. I may have to take the classes again, but I am willing to do that if he requires that I do so." Levi glanced over at Emily in time to see her eyes widen in surprise.

"Are you ready to do that?"

"*Jah*, I am. I am never leaving again, Emmy. This is *mie* home and I want to be baptized into the church, so I can be a respected member of the community." He told her.

"That is *wunderbaar*, Levi." She smiled brightly.

Just seeing her sweet smile caused his heart to beat double time. Even though making her happy wasn't the main reason he was being baptized, he *liebed* her so much and he was glad she was pleased with his decision.

Chapter Six

"I hope your *familye* will not be upset with me for not *kuming* to see them while you were gone." Emily sighed.

They will not be, they *lieb* you Emmy."

Emily was a little nervous as Levi helped her down from the

buggy. She prayed he was right and they wouldn't be upset with her that she had not *kume* to see them, or participated in any of the quilting bee's, at their *haus* while Levi had been gone.

"Don't be nervous." Levi tried to reassure her that everything would be okay. They walked into his kitchen and Levi greeted his *mamm*, *daed* and *familye*. Emily noticed they were all home tonight and they all greeted her, smiled and made her feel comfortable. She had always liked Levi's *familye* and she was glad they did not seem upset with her

Karen, Levi's *mamm* said, "it is so *gut* to see you, Emily. We are glad you could join us this evening. Please sit at the table and make yourself comfortable, supper is ready. Levi seated Emily next to him and then everyone pulled out their chairs and sat down as well. Gideon, Levi's *daed,* bowed his head and everyone followed as he said the silent prayer over the evening meal. He cleared his throat to let everyone know he was finished and then started the dishes around the table. Everyone served themselves and then the meal began. Emily enjoyed supper and visiting with Levi's family. They made her feel at home and she was relieved that the entire evening went well, as she helped *redd up* the kitchen.

Before they left, Karen said, "Emily, we are so glad you could join us this evening and will see you at the barn raising in the morning."

"*Danke*, Karen and for the *wunderbaar* meal." She smiled.

"Welkom." She returned her smile.

On the way back to her *haus,* Emily looked over at Levi. "That went better than I thought it would. Your *familye* was so gracious and seemed to be happy to see me."

"They *lieb* you, they were happy to have you join us and they are pleased we are seeing each other again."

"That is *gut,* I am glad. I *lieb* them too. I hope and pray Bishop Yoder will agree to let you be baptized."

"I am sure that he will. He is a very kind man and he wants us to all stay here in the community, so I believe he will be happy that I am home to stay."

Levi took Emmy home and walked her to the door. Would it

be all right if I pick you up for the barn raising in the morning?"

"*Jah*, I would like that." She smiled up at him.

******

It was all Levi could do to not lean down and kiss her right there on her porch steps, but he knew it would not be appropriate this soon. "*Guder Nacht*, Emmy. I will see you in the morning then. Sleep well." He waited while she opened the door.

"*Guder Nacht*, Levi. *Danke* for the nice evening. " She smiled and went inside. He walked out to his buggy, stepped up and backed Leo out onto the road to head home. He would be glad when morning got here.

Saturday morning dawned bright and sunny but cold. Emily

Mamm, Nancy, Brenda and Susan had been cooking and baking since four a.m. for the barn raising. Emily was excited about seeing her friends and Levi would be picking her up today. She could enjoy being around him even though it would be at a distance most of the day, since he would be helping build the barn.

"I can't believe I'm going to get to spend the whole day with, Jacob, even though there will be lots of other folks around, it will still be nice." Nancy grinned.

Emily smiled at her younger *schweschder's* enthusiasm. She was happy Nancy had found such a nice responsible young man. Levi's younger *bruder* would make Nancy a *gut* husband in a year or so. Emily hugged her. "I'm glad you have found someone who makes you happy, but how can you tell him and Joshua apart?"

"I have always been able to tell them apart." Nancy grinned. Jacob is very responsible, kind and easy going. Joshua is responsible too but he is really quiet. He hardly says a word. They are both very kind and caring, but Jacob is the one who caught my attention. They have different personalities, but most twins do.".

"Well, I am glad you can." Emily shook her head, "I have never been able to figure out which one is which. I do not think I would want to be with someone that I wasn't sure I had the right one."

Nancy laughed. "Very funny, Believe me you would know. Now we better help *Mamm* before she gets unhappy with us standing around. The frown disappeared replaced by another grin."

"*Jah*, that's for sure and certain, cause if *mamm's* not happy, ain't nobody happy."They said in unison and laughed together. They carried the food out to the buggy, so they could take it to the barn raising.

They had just finished loading the dishes into *daed's* buggy, when Levi pulled in.

"Levi stepped down and walked over to Emily and Nancy.

"*Wie Ghets?*"

"*Gut, danke.*" Emily smiled.

"Are you ready to go?"

"*Jah.*" She turned and said. "Nancy, I will see you at *mammi* and *daadi's.*" Emily hugged her younger *schweschder* and let Levi help her into the buggy. She waved as they backed out onto the road and headed for her *grosseldre's farmhaus*.

"While you are helping *redd* up after the barn raising, Emmy. I will meet with Bishop Yoder and I should be finished by the time you are ready to go home."

"*Danke*, I will wait if you aren't quite through by the time I am." She smiled. "I will be praying for you."

"*Danke, leibchen*. I appreciate that." He smiled.

Chapter Seven

Emma served *kaffi,* water, or
lemonade, to the men as they
worked. She handed Levi a glass
of water and he smiled and
thanked her. She smiled back and
her heart ached. If he had just
stayed instead of leaving on

Rumspringa, things between them would be so different, they would be married by now. *Emily stop thinking that way, if Levi had not gone he would never have been happy,* she scolded herself and then prayed they could still be together in the future. She went to the next man working and on down the line, serving each one his choice of beverage.

Around noon they served a meal, with the men being served first and once they were finished the women and then children were served, which was always the way things were done with the plain people. Emily was standing beside Nancy filling her plate, when the wind caught it and almost knocked it out of her hand. She needed to concentrate on what she was doing instead of watching Levi. She joined Rebekah, Emily's best friend, Nancy and Deborah, Levi's *schweschder* which was, Nancy's best friend, at one of the tables.

"Emily, I was waiting for you to join us to tell my news."

The excitement on Nancy's face gave it away before she said anything, but Emily pretended she hadn't noticed. "What news? I'm here now, tell us." Emily grinned at her younger *schweschder*.

"You have to promise to keep it between the four of us." Nancy's excitement was contagious.

"We will, now tell us." Emily laughed along with Rebekah and Deborah.

"Jacob asked me to marry him during wedding season next year." She treated them to a bright smile.

"That is *wunderbaar* news,

s*chweschder*. Jacob is a *gut, honest mann* and he'll make you a *gut* husband." Emily leaned over and hugged Nancy, so happy that her little *schweschder* had made a good match. Her future was set and Emily was thrilled for her.

"We will," Nancy smiled, but Emily, Levi is a *gut* man too and he still cares for you, it is obvious when he looks at you."

"*Danke*, Nancy. I appreciate you saying that." Emily turned and headed for the *haus*. Just as she stepped into the hall, she overheard Ellen Belier in the kitchen say,

"Levi Graber is back. I hope he is going to the singing tomorrow night. I want to try to get him to notice me, so maybe he will ask to take me home in his buggy." She smiled at her friend.

"Ellen, you are going to get hurt if you set your sights on Levi Graber. He is so hung up on Emily Mast, he cannot see anyone else." Naomi King told her friend.

"He was before he left, but maybe he has changed his mind, it never hurts to try." Ellen smiled as they walked out of the room.

Would Levi be interested in Ellen? Emily waited until they had gone back outside before she went on into the kitchen. *Ack,* Levi. Emily's heart began to pound, what if Ellen was there and Levi found he *was* interested in her?" Emily felt sick at just the thought that he might be. Well, right now she didn't have time to dwell on it; she needed to help *redd up* the kitchen, so she would be ready when Levi came to take her home.

A little while later Emily had

just finished with the kitchen when Levi walked in. "Are you ready?" He smiled.

"*Jah,* She removed the apron she had been using and hung it up before joining him. They walked out to the buggy and he helped her up onto the seat, before going around and joining her. When he had backed up and headed out onto the road toward her *haus,* he glanced over at her.

"Are you all right? You seem upset?"

"I am all right. How did your meeting go?" She quickly changed the subject. She was not going to tell him what she had overheard in the kitchen.

"It went well, I am going to be baptized in the morning." He grinned.

"In the morning?" She asked

surprised.

"*Jah,* Bishop Yoder said since I had completed the classes, there was no need for me to repeat them. He has a class being baptized in the morning, so he asked if I would like to join them and I was surprised but pleased, so I quickly agreed."

"That is *wunderbaar*, Levi. I am so happy for you."

"*Danke, Emmy.*"

Levi pulled over underneath a tree. He prayed it wasn't too soon but he had to talk to Emmy.

"Why are we stopping? Emmy glanced at him.

"I would like to talk to you without any interruptions." He looked at her for a moment. "Emmy, *Ich lieb dich* with all *mie* heart. I am so sorry I left and I will never leave you again. After I am baptized tomorrow, would you consider courting me and I would like in future for you to be me *fraa*?" Levi waited anxiously for her to answer.

"Levi," she looked over at him.

He was afraid she was going to turn him down and his heart pounded in dread. What would he do if she did? He did not want to spend his future without her in his life. He would be devastated.

"Levi," she said again catching his attention.

He looked at her and waited anxiously for her to continue.

"Ich lieb dich too and I would *lieb* to court you. I would in time *lieb* to be your *fraa* as well, but let us give ourselves some courting time before we talk about a date for a wedding."

Levi was so relieved she did

not say *nee*, he was willing to wait for a wedding date, as long as they could be together. "That is *gut*, Emmy. I am happy to be courting you and I will wait for us to set a wedding date, *danke*." He smiled and she smiled back.

"As much as I would like to stay right here with you, I guess I better take you home, so your *mamm* and *daed* will not wonder where you are. He pulled back onto the road. When they arrived at Emmy's *haus* Levi pulled up in front of her door. He jumped down and came around to help her. She placed her hand in his and he assisted her to the ground and walked her to the kitchen door.

"I will see you in the morning at service and I will look forward to seeing you be baptized. Nothing could make me happier than to know you will be a baptized member and staying here." Emmy smiled up at him."

"*Danke*, Emmy. I am looking forward to it too and I am glad you are happy. I will try to always make you happy. *Ich lieb dich* and I will see you in the morning."

"*Ich lieb dich* too. Have a *gut* afternoon."She said and went inside.

Levi went back out and climbed into his buggy to head home.

Chapter Eight

Sunday morning dawned overcast and cold. After breakfast, Emily went upstairs to get her heavy winter coat. She slipped her coat on and the bonnet over her prayer *kapp* before heading back down stairs. As Emily came into the kitchen *mamm* was putting her bonnet on. "*Ich lieb dich, Mamm.*"

"*Ich lieb dich, Dochder.*" *Mamm* hugged her. "Your *daed* and *bruders* went out to hitch the buggy. Are you ready?"

"*Jah*, Emily picked up the chicken noodle casserole she her *schweschders* had helped *Mamm* fix the day before. Nancy took the lemon cake, and they all went out to the buggy. *Daed* smiled at them and helped *Mamm* onto the front seat, before he took the seat next to her. John, Nancy, Steven, Brenda, Susan and Micah, piled into the back. Emily sat next to *Mamm* in the front. When *Daed* looked her way and smiled, Emily smiled back.

Daed flicked the reins and Boaz started off on the drive to the neighbors for the morning church service. Emily had always enjoyed the familiar clip-clop of the horse's hooves against the pavement and now was no different, it was a comforting sound. She had missed Levi so much it would be so nice to have him in church services. She just prayed this morning that all of their neighbors would be kind, once they realized Levi was back to stay and be happy he was being baptized into the church. Her thoughts were interrupted a few minutes later when her *Daed* pulled the buggy into the Bontrager's driveway. James Bontrager's youngest *sohn*, Isaac, took the reins from *Daed* and offered to unhitch and water the horse. *Daed* thanked him and helped *Mamm* from the buggy.

John jumped down and offered Emily a hand. Steven helped Nancy, Leah and Susan after he and Micah jumped down.

"*Danki*, John." Emma gave her *bruder* a smile and followed her parents into James Bontrager's *haus*. The women took the dishes for the meal, following service, into the kitchen and added them to the many others sitting on the counter. The men went into the large room where church would be held.

The Bontrager's living room was packed to the edges with backless benches. Some on one side of the room and the rest on the other side, with an open aisle down the middle separating them. Emily, Nancy, Brenda, Susan and *Mamm* found a seat on the women's side. Emily noticed Levi sitting next to Jacob and Joshua, his younger twin *bruders*, on one of the benches on the men's side, across the room. He and his *bruder's* were talking, so he didn't notice Emily at first. A few minutes later when their eyes met, Levi smiled warmly and then turned back to continue his conversation.

"*Wie gehts*?" Rebekah slid onto the bench on the other side of Emily.

"Nervous for Levi, but otherwise I'm okay. I'm so glad you are here. The men nodded to him, but no one has spoken to him that I have seen. I guess I shouldn't be surprised, he has been gone for a year. They are probably a little leery of his decision and wonder if he will stay."

"They will *kume* around in time. I wouldn't worry, it's going to be okay, you'll see."

"*Danki,* Rebekah. I appreciate your support.

"I will always support you."

"*Danke*, I will for you as well." She smiled.

Emily glanced in Levi's direction again and noticed he was listening to something his *bruder* was telling him. She wondered what they were talking about. She glanced around and at the other end of the bench, where she was sitting, was Ellen Beiler. She was smiling in Levi's direction. Emily glanced that way just in time to see Levi smile back at her. Emily froze in her seat, was Levi interested in Ellen? Surely not. He wouldn't have asked her to court him and marry him in the future, if he was interested in Ellen, would he?

"Are you all right?" Rebekah whispered next to her.

"Did you notice that Ellen Beiler and Levi were exchanging smiles?"

"*Jah*, she may be interested in him, but everyone knew how he felt about you when he left, including her and he obviously still feels about you, or he wouldn't be wanting to see you again. I believe he was just polite by smiling back at her, but that doesn't mean he's interested in her. Levi has always smiled politely at all the *maedels* when he greeted them. Let's not jump to conclusions here."

Emily prayed Rebekah was right. Movement across the room caught her attention. The Bishop and ministers were going into the room across from them to decide who would bring the message this morning. Before long, they would return and Levi along with all the others who had completed the class, would be taken into the other room while the congregation sang. Once the meeting was completed, they would rejoin the congregation for the main message. She looked once more at Levi and their eyes met again, as he smiled warmly at her.

Emily glanced over at Ellen and caught her scowling. Obviously, Ellen had seen Levi looking at Emily and she wasn't happy. Before she had any more time to think about it, the Bishop called Levi and the others to follow him into the room next door.

Levi followed the Bishop and the other candidates for baptism into the back. Once they were seated, Levi tried to relax as the singing started in the other room. He listened to Bishop Yoder for the next half hour, as he gave them instructions for their baptism. As the class finished and the bishop closed in prayer Levi, closed his eyes and listened to the many voices in the next room and enjoyed the soothing sound. A few minutes later, they joined the service with the rest of the congregation. The Bishop gave the message this morning and Levi really enjoyed being back in service once again. He had not realized until now, how much he had miss worshipping with this congregation, of family and friends.

Bishop Yoder stood before the congregation. "I have something I would like to share with you before we close the service. I feel Levi Graber is sincere in his feelings and desire to be a part of us once again. He went out on *Rumspringa* for a period of time, but now he is ready to live plain and abide by the *Ordnung*. We are a forgiving people and we need to, love and welcome Levi into our church and community. I have agreed to allow him to take the baptism, due to his completion of the baptismal classes, he attended just before he left last year. He will be baptized this morning with the group, who have just completed their classes." Bishop Troyer smiled at Levi and called all of the candidates for Baptism to come forward and kneel, which they did. After each candidate answered all of the questions. Each one was baptized in the name of the Father, Son and Holy Spirit. After the women received a holy kiss by the Bishops wife, Bishop Yoder closed in prayer." The men received several pats on the back including Levi, as he was welcomed back into the Community.

Chapter Nine

Emily went into the kitchen to help serve the meal. When it was the women's turn to eat, after helping serve, Emily sat with Rebekah and Nancy. She had just filled her plate when Levi and

Jacob sat down across from them. "Are you *maedels* going to the singing this evening?" Jacob asked, before taking a bite of his food.

"I plan to go. Nancy smiled. " Emily, Rebekah are you going?"

Rebekah looked at Emily. "I plan to go. Are you going Emily?"

"*Jah*, I believe I will." She smiled.

"Levi what about you, are you going tonight?" Jacob asked.

"Levi looked at his *bruder* and then at Emily and grinned. "*Jah,* I I plan to go too."

"Emma was excited about going to the singing again, it had been so long since they last went and she had missed being there with Levi.

"Well, I need to get home and do some chores before I go

tonight. I'll see all of you later then." Levi waved as he left."I better go too and help." Jacob smiled at Nancy.

"I'll see you *maedels* this evening."Emily smiled to herself at the dreamy expression on Nancy's face. She was happy her *schweschder* was going to be able to marry the *mann* she loved.

With the meals all served and the dishes finished, Emily climbed into the buggy with her *familye*. When they pulled up to the barn, *Daed* said, "*Buwe's* would you take care of Boaz and put the buggy away and check on the pups, before you *kume* inside?"

"We'll take care of it, *Daed,*" *John* said. Steven and Micah nodded and followed their *bruder*.

Once the *buwes* were inside the haus," *Daed* stood beside Emma.

"I'm not pleased about Levi leaving the way he did, but your *mamm* and I *lieb you.* You are our *dochder* and we want you to be happy. We are pleased that Levi took the baptismal classes and is going to stay in our community. He came to talk to me after service this morning and said he *liebed* you and wanted to ask for your hand in marriage soon. He wanted our blessing, we gave it to him and we are giving it to you. We *lieb* you and we can see how much you *lieb* him. We want you to be happy. We are pleased that you are back to attending the things going on in the community once again."

Tears filled Emily's eyes and rolled down her face. She wiped them away with the back of her hand. "I'm so sorry, *Daed*, I never meant to hurt you and *mamm* or any of you, by staying in *mie* room and closing *mieself* off from all of you and the community." She looked at her *schweschders* and *bruders*. "I know now I should never have done that, but I was so devastated when Levi left, I made a bad decision. I want to try to do everything I can, to make up to you all for the worry I've caused."Despite her best efforts to control herself, she began to sob. All of the hurt she had bottled up this last year came to the surface

"Do not cry so, *dochder*, we are relieved that you are out of your room and happy once again. We love you. *Daed* drew her into his arms and hugged her. 'Now dry your tears."

"*Danki*, I *lieb* all of you too." *Danke, Gott*. Emily prayed. She was so thankful Levi was home to stay and her world was back to normal once again.

******

Levi grabbed his jacket and headed downstairs.

"*Sohn*, are you going to the singing tonight?" *Mamm* asked."

"*Jah*, I was just getting ready to leave." Levi grabbed his hat from the hook. He kissed *Mamm* on the cheek and headed out to his buggy. Levi's feelings for Emily were just as strong as they were the day she left. He was so thankful her *daed* and *mamm* had given him their blessing this morning. When the time was right he intended to ask her to marry him. In the mean time he had saved most of the money he had made while he was gone and he was going to see if he could find some land and build him and Emily a *haus*.

Chapter Ten

"Emily, if you are going to the singing this evening you need to ride with your *bruder*. I don't want you out at night by yourself. John is going to take Pete to pull the buggy, you can go with him."

Daed took a bite of the shoofly pie *mamm* had sat in front of him.

"Gabriel and Rebekah are *kuming* to take me, *Daed*. Rebekah's *daed* wouldn't allow her to go alone at night either, so her *bruder* offered to take us both."

"That is *gut*. If you *maedel* are with Gabriel, I will not worry. He is a fine young man and he will make sure you get home safe."

When a knock sounded at the kitchen door a few minutes later Emily answered it and opened the screen. "*Kume* in." She stepped back and Gabriel and Rebekah followed her into the kitchen.

"Gideon, Rebekah. *Wie gehts*?" Faith asked.

"We're *gut, danki*." Gabriel answered for both of them and Rebekah nodded her agreement.

"Would you like a piece of pie and a cup of *kaffi* before you go?"

"*Ack, nee, danki,* not for me," Gabriel said, "we will be eating at the singing." He smiled.

"Rebekah?" Faith asked.

"N*ee, danki*, Faith, Not for me either." Rebekah smiled.

"You *kinner* have a *gut* time, but be careful," *Daed* said. "*Danki,* Gabriel, for taking the *maedels.*"

"*Welkom* and we will be careful, Noah. I'll bring them back home safe." Gabriel reassured *daed* before they left.

Gabriel helped Emily and Rebekah into the buggy before stepping up himself. He backed up and headed to the Bontrager's farm for the singing.

Once they arrived, Isaac took the reins and offered to take care of Clara, so Gabriel followed the *maedels* inside.

Emily sat next to Rebekah, on a bench outside the barn that had been set up for that purpose.

"I'm a little nervous about being here tonight," Emily admitted with a sigh.

"Why? You've been to lots of youth gatherings."

"I know, but It's been a year since I was here."

"Jah, but everyone will be glad that you are out of your room and *kuming* again." Some of the *maedels* Emily and Rebekah had gone to *schul* with, came by and welcomed Emily back to the singings. She was grateful. After the *maedels* left to find a seat, she and Rebekah watched several of the *buwes*, including Levi, Jacob, Joshua, and John, play softball, which was traditional."Rebekah, is there anyone here you interested in seeing?" Emily glanced at her friend.

"*Nee*, there is not anyone here I am interested in seeing." Rebekah stated.

Emily glanced over at her *frienden*, there are lots of nice young *menner* that would make you a *gut* husband. I have noticed several smiling at you this evening."

"*Jah* and they are nice enough, but I'm not interested. They can make another *maedel* a *gut* husband, but it will not be me."

"Is there someone else that is not here that you're interested in?" Emily asked.

"Emily noticed Rebekah hesitated before answering, I am not in any hurry to give up *mie* freedom. Maybe one of these days I will, now that I am baptized." Rebekah smiled at Emily.

Okay, I get the message we will drop it for now." Emily watched Ellen Beiler try to get Levi's attention.

"She may be interested in him, but he hasn't shown any interest in her," Rebekah whispered.

"I surely hope he does not, since just between you and me, he asked to court me yesterday afternoon after the barn raising." She grinned.

"*Ack*, that is *wunderbaar*, Emily." I am so happy for you."

"*Danke*, Emily was relieved when Levi smiled at the other *maedel*, but didn't show any interest.

"It doesn't look to me like Ellen is having any success, with attracting Levi's attention."

Emily squeezed Rebekah's hand. "I am so blessed, what did I ever do to deserve a *frienden* like you?" She gave her a smile.

"*Ack*, I do not know, probably the same thing I did to deserve a *frienden* like you, nothing, but the *gut* Lord gave us each other anyway and I thank Him every day for you."Rebekah grinned.

"Emily smiled, "*Jah* and I thank him for you too. You always know what to say to make me feel better when I'm upset and *Ich lieb dich* for it. *Danke*."

"*Welkom* and you me. Not to change the subject, but look who has attracted Levi's attention now." Rebekah gently bumped shoulders with Emily.

"Emily glanced his way and found him looking right at her. He smiled and she smiled back, before he turned away to finish playing the game. Emily glanced up and noticed Ellen glaring at her before she stomped off.

"*Ack*, someone is not happy that Levi only has eyes for you." Rebekah said. "Let's move over by the bond fire. Now that the sun has gone down it's getting cold."

"*Jah*, you're right it is. The fire will feel *gut*." Emily followed Rebekah over to where hay bales had been positioned, several feet back from the fire in a circle. The *buwes* and *maedels* sat on opposite sides. Levi, Jacob Joshua's *frienden,* Jonah and Elijah Yoder, the Bishop's *sohn,* had just walked in, and sat next to Levi. They all sat right across from her, Rebekah, Nancy, Deborah, Levi's schweschder and Ellen beside

Naomi. Everyone started to sing and Emily realized just how much she had missed this as she joined in with the others to praise the Lord. When the singing came to an end Emily and Rebekah made their way into the barn along with everyone else to share snacks and have fellowship. Levi and Elijah had been visiting quite a lot since Elijah came in this evening, Emily had noticed. They had been close before Levi left. Now that he was back, she prayed they could build that close friendship again. A few moments later Levi and Elijah made their way over to where Emily and Rebekah were sitting with their plates of food.

"Is it okay if we sit here? When they both nodded, they sat down with Levi across from Emily and Elijah sat across from

Rebekah, a plate of food in both their hands.

"Levi asked, Emmy, are you going to the auction next Saturday?"He took a bite of his sandwich.

"*Jah*, I told *Mamm* I would help with our table. Are you going?"

"*Jah,* I'll be going along with *Daed, mamm, mie bruders and schweschders.*

"Rebekah, are you going? Elijah asked her.

"She glanced at him and said, "*Jah, mie familye* has a table also. Will you be going?" She smiled.

"*Jah,* I will be there to help *mie familye* as well." He smiled back.

Emily could hardly believe it. Rebekah had not showed any interest in anyone, but she

obviously cared for Elijah Yoder.
This was the first singing he had
attended. Nancy always shared
with Emily who was there each
time and she had commented
Elijah never came, hadn't in
several months, yet he was here
tonight. That was interesting.

Chapter Eleven

"Have you been by to see the new *schul*, Levi?" Rebekah asked him.

"*Nee*, I haven't yet. Has it been completed now?"

"*Jah*, Rebekah answered. We had two fund raisers this last year.

We prepared supper both times and opened them to the communities in the area. We raised enough to complete the *schul* and to buy books. It is a *wunderbaar schul for our kinner*." She grinned. "Miriam, *mie* older *schweschder*, is the teacher now.

"That is *gut*. We needed a *schul*. I will make sure to go by to see it soon." Levi assured her as he picked up the last of his sandwich, they we all about finished and they would be heading home from the singing soon. He was glad he came he had missed being here with Emmy and all of his *frienden*.

******

"It was a *gut* singing, *Jah?*" Rebekah sat her drink on the floor beside her. "Emily, aren't you glad now that you came?"

"*Jah*, I have realized how much I have missed it, I am glad I came, I've enjoyed it. She glanced at Levi and he smiled.

"I am glad you did too. Would it be all right if I take you home tonight?" He asked.

"Emily looked at him and smiled."*Jah,* I would like that.

"*Gut.*" he smiled back as they finished their meal. "We should go pretty soon, it's getting late."

"Rebecca, I am going to ride home with Levi. *Danke* for bringing me."

"*Welkom*, she smiled.

Would you like for me to take your empty plates?"

"*Danki,*" Emily, Rebekah and Deborah said and handed him their plates, but, Emily noticed Elijah took Rebekah's and she smiled at him. Jacob had already taken Nancy's and she had agreed to ride home with him.

Emily realized that Ellen had agreed to ride home with Jonah since Levi had asked Emily to ride home with him and Rebekah had not shown any interest in any of the *menner* tonight, until Elijah decided to join them. *Please Gott if Elijah is the mate you have chosen for Rebekah, I pray they will be happy"* Emily prayed.

Levi returned from throwing away their plates and asked Emily, are you ready to go?"

"*Jah*, I am. *Guder nacht.* Everyone. Rebekah, I will see you at work tomorrow.*"*

******

Levi said *guder nacht* to everyone as they were all getting ready to leave and told Elijah, "It was *gut* seeing you again."

"Elijah nodded. It was *gut* seeing you too, *mie frienden*. It has been too long." He smiled.

Levi waited for Emmy to stand up, helped her with her coat and then she was ready to go with him, for which he was pleased. He prayed as he walked her to his buggy and helped her up onto the seat. Thanking *Gott* for allowing them to have another chance for a future together. Once she was settled and had a warm quilt over her legs, he stepped up onto the seat next to her. He backed his buggy out of the driveway onto the road, heading toward her *haus*. "Are you warm enough?"

"Jah, danke.

"Levi was happy to be here with Emily, in his buggy after the singing on their way to her *haus* together. *Danke again Gott, for*

bringing me home and letting us get back together."

"Are you sure you're warm enough? There's another quilt in the back if you need it." Levi glanced at her.

"*Jah*, I am fine. These quilts are plenty warm, *danke,*" Emily answered. When she smiled at him, his heart nearly skipped a beat, he *liebed* her so much.

"Would you go to supper with me tomorrow after work?"

"*Jah*, I would like that. She smiled.

"*Gut*, there is something I want to share with you. I do not want any secrets between us ever. I will always be open and honest with you. *Ich lieb dich* so much and I want to share with you everything I experienced while I was gone, on *Rumspringa.*"

"Alright, and I will always be open and honest with you as well."

"I will pick you up at 5:30pm if that is okay tomorrow."

"*Jah*, that will be *gut*. I will look forward to our time together." She smiled as he pulled into her driveway and parked in front of her kitchen door. He stepped out and came around to help her down. He walked her up onto the porch and placed a quick kiss on her soft lips, "*Ich lieb dich. Guder Nacht,* I will see you tomorrow, sleep well *Leibchen.*"

"*Ich lieb dich, too. Guder Nacht,* Levi." She smiled and went into the *haus*.

******

The next morning Levi helped milk. When he, his *daed* and *bruders* went into the kitchen for breakfast, there was a young woman sitting at the kitchen table and she had an infant carrier sitting on the floor next to her. His *daed* looked at his *mamm* for an explanation and then told the *buwes* to go wash up for breakfast. Levi was concerned at the expression on his *mamm's* face. She was obviously very upset with whatever this young woman had told her. Levi sat down at the table as his *bruders* came back and took their chairs.

Mamm said, as they were all seated, "I will let this Miss Chambers explain after breakfast, why she is here."

Levi glanced at the woman sitting at their table and looked again at the infant seat on the floor next to her, that was covered by a blanket.

Once the meal was finished, *daed* said, "*buwes* please go and open the store. Your *bruder* and I will follow soon. *Maedels* please *redd* up the kitchen while your *mamm, bruder* and I move to the front room to speak with Miss Chambers. They moved to the front room and Levi was a little uncomfortable. Since his parents included him in this conversation, he was sure this woman was here to speak about something that concerned him. His concerns were brought to light when the woman's voice caught his attention.

"I have come to speak to you, Levi," she looked at him.

Levi studied her for a moment He knew he had never seen her before, so what could she possibly want to speak to him about? "I am sorry, have we met? I apologize, but I do not remember ever seeing you before."

"No, we have not met, but we had a mutual acquaintance."

"A mutual acquaintance? Who might that be?" He questioned.

"Do you remember meeting Macy Benton at a party last year on New Year's Eve ?"

"Levi took a deep breath and his heart began to pound at her words. He swallowed before he answered. "*Jah*, I remember Macy. I met her that night at the party."

Chapter Twelve

"Well, Macy was a good friend of mine. She had a heart condition and when she found out she was carry a child, the doctor told her she would not survive child birth, but she refused to terminate the pregnancy."

"She was carrying a child?" Levi closed his eyes for a moment before he opened them and looked at her, he knew what this woman was going to say next. *Dear Gott, What have I done?*

"Yes, Levi, she was carrying your child."

He heard his *mamm* and *daed* both gasp. "Levi, what is the meaning of this? I believe you had better explain." *Daed* insisted.

"I will explain, *daed,* but first I must say, I did not know. Levi looked at Macy's friend. He felt about half sick.

"I know you didn't. Macy told me she did not tell you. She only lived two hours after the baby was born. Long enough to name her child and to fill out the birth Certificate."

She looked up at him and the pain in her light blue eyes wrenched his heart. "Are you all right?" he asked gently.

After a moment she nodded and continued. "She told me you were the baby's father and gave me your name and where I could find you. She made me promise I would bring her baby to you. She said you were so kind. She knew you were Amish and felt her daughter would be loved, well cared for and raised to know the Lord. So I promised to bring the baby to you and now she is your baby."

"She? The *boppli* is a girl?" Levi managed to choke out against the lump that had formed in his throat. He was a *daed*. What was he going to do? How was he going to explain this to his parents and to

Emmy?

Miss Chambers lifted the *boppli* from the infant carrier and handed her to Levi. He looked at her as if she had lost her mind. He did not know that much about *boppli's*, what was he going to do?

Even with the shock they were experiencing *mamm* and *daed* could not resist *kuming* over to look at their first *grandkinner*. Levi looked at the tiny *boppli's* face, Miss Chambers handed to him and his heart softened. As he looked down at her, he knew without a doubt she was his *dochder,* even though he did not remember anything about that night. He felt as if he'd been hit in the chest with a sledge hammer, he couldn't seem to get enough air all of a sudden. He finally recovered enough to look at her again. What little hair she had was the color of wheat and her eyes, which were open and looking at him, were already turning green just like his, his *daed* and *siblings*. It was a Graber trait, they all had green eyes and hair the color of wheat. He fell in *lieb* with her immediately. She was his *dochder* for sure and certain. He slid a slightly shaking hand through his light hair, taking a minute to compose himself.

"We were not even sure we had, had such contact." Levi swallowed and hesitated for a minute before he said anymore. "*Mie frienden* talked me into going to this party. They said if I was going to experience *Rumspringa*, I must go to a New Years Eve party. I should never have gone, but they just wouldn't take *nee* for an answer. Do not get me wrong, I made the decision to go with them, so this is on me not *mie frienden.* I met Macy that evening when we sat at the same table with her. We shared several glasses of punch and talked for quite some time. That is all I remember until the next morning. When I woke up I was in bed next to Macy. Neither one of us could remember anything after drinking the last glass of punch. We had no idea how we came to be there in the bedroom, much less in the same bed together. I told Macy I was sorry for us being there together, even though I did not remember how we got there and she said she did not remember either. He ran a shaky hand through his hair again.

I got up and went into the

bathroom to get dressed and when I came out Macy was gone. No one seemed to know how to find her. *Mie frienden* told me later that morning, that the punch had rum in it. I had never drank alcohol. I knew it tasted different than anything I had ever had before, but I never dreamed alcohol was the reason for it. Then I realized why we did not remember anything that night."

"That is the exactly what Macy told me after she found out she was going to have a baby. She had never drank alcohol either. She was a Christian and never went to parties. She said her friend she was traveling with for work, talked her into going with her."

"I am sorry for ever agreeing to go to that party and I am sorry about, Macy. She seemed like a nice *maedel* and I would never have allowed this to happen, had I realized the punch was spiked, I believe is what *mie frienden* called it." Levi glanced down at his *dochder.*

"Well obviously this was an unfortunate set of circumstances you both found yourselves in," Miss Chambers said, but this precious little one needs to be loved and taken care of."

"*Jah*, I agree. It is no fault of hers that this happened. Before he could say anymore, Miss Chambers made a comment and he looked up.

"I have to take a sample for a DNA test, which is just a swab of the inside of your mouth. Even though we know the baby is yours, we have to have proof legally, before I can leave her with you. If you will open your mouth I will take a sample. It will take a couple of days to get the results back. When I have them, I will bring the baby back to you, with a copy of the DNA results and her birth Certificate for your records.

Levi opened his mouth and she swabbed the inside of his jaw, with what looked like a one ended Qtip. She then placed it in a bag, sealed it and reached to take the *boppli* from *mamm. L*evi had handed the *boppli* to his mother, while Miss Chambers swabbed his mouth. She laid Katie back in the carrier and said have a *gut* day."

Daed walked her to the back and opened the door for her as she left.

Chapter Thirteen

When *daed* rejoined them in the front room, Levi looked at him and then at *mamm*. "I am so sorry. I should never have gone on *Rumspringa*. I never dreamed something like this would happen. Macy has lost her life because of *mie* poor decision and I am heart sick about that. This *boppli* is mine. I have no doubt after seeing her, that she is *mie dochder* and I will take *mie* responsibility and raise her. I asked *Gott* for forgiveness that morning, in case we were in fact together. I told Bishop Yoder of this before I knew about Katie. He said, this was unfortunate, but it happened before I was baptized, so I did not need to confess before the church. Levi shook his head, he was devastated. "What am I going to tell Emily?"

"*Sohn*, the Bishop is correct, this is an unfortunate thing that has happened." *Daed* shook his head as well, "but it cannot be changed now and this *maedel's* death is not your burden to bear, it was Gott's will. We are a *familye* and we are here for you."

"*Sohn*, you are correct that this should never have happened *mamm* agreed, "but it did and your *daed* is right, it cannot be changed. We are human and we make mistakes. Attending that party was clearly a mistake, that is why we need *Gott* in our lives and He is very forgiving. If it turns out you are Katie's *daed*, we will take her into our *familye* and she will be part of us. You must go talk to Emily before she hears this from someone else and we will be praying."

"I am taking Emily out for the evening meal after work and I will talk to her then. I know this is going to be hard for her. I promised her I would never do anything to hurt her again. I meant those words when I said them, but

I did not expect this to happen after all this time. Since I had not heard anything from Macy, I was hoping maybe we did not have contact after all." He dropped his head into his hands for a minute before he said, "I already told Emily I had something I needed to tell her, that I did not want any secrets between us. I had intended to share this with her and I have been praying she could forgive me for that night. I did not know whether we were even together at that time, but now there is no doubt, so she may not want anything to do with me."

"*Sohn*, Emily *liebs* you, it was obvious last night when she was here in the way she looked at you, but it may take time for her to be able to deal with this news."

"I pray you're right *mamm*

and *that* she can, it is a lot to deal with and it goes against our beliefs."

"We all make mistakes, *Sohn.* We have to ask *Gott* for forgiveness and learn from them." *Mamm* told him.

Danke, Daed, Mamm, I appreciate your support and your forgiveness. I *lieb* you both. When I asked *Gott* for His forgiveness, I know that he also forgave me. I pray He will work this out and Emily will be able to find it in her heart to forgive me as well."

"We will be praying also and we *lieb* you too *sohn.*" *Mamm* hugged him.

"We better to go to the shop and help the *buwes.*" *Daed* stood and grabbed his hat from the rack and Levi did the same.

"We will continue to pray,

sohn.

"*Danke*, that means a lot, just knowing you are both praying."

It seemed to Levi that the day passed by very slowly. He could not get his mind off of their visitor that morning and how he was going to explain it to Emily. He was glad when his *daadi* and *daed* came out onto the floor, where he and his *bruders* had been working on furniture pieces all day.

"It is time to go home *buwes*. We have put in a *gut* day." *Daed* told them.

They cleaned up all of their tools and closed the store.

"I will be home later *Daed,* I am picking Emily up to go to supper in town."

"We will be praying for you

Sohn, Gott will work this out. We will see you at the *haus* later this evening."

"*Danke, Daed.*"Levi went out to the small barn, secured Leo to the buggy and climbed up into the driver's seat. He backed out of the small barn behind the store and headed to Emily's *haus*. "Please *Gott,* I made a mistake and I know what I did was wrong, but I believe you have forgiven me. I ask that you would please work this out between me and Emily and please be with little Katie." Levi prayed as he pulled up into Emily's driveway and parked his buggy in front of her door. He jumped down, walked up to her *haus* and knocked. He *liebed* her so much and he knew what he was going to tell her was going to devastate her. Just the thought of hurting her crushed him, but there was no way around it. He wished he had never gone on *Rumspringa*, but he could not change the past. He would just have to deal with the repercussions from it and he was not looking forward to it. He hoped and prayed once she heard what he had to say, that she could forgive him. He looked up as the door opened. She looked amazing as usual. The blue dress she was wearing made her eyes even bluer if that was possible.

"*Wie Ghets*, Levi." She smiled and stepped out onto the porch. "*Gut danke, Wie Ghets*?" He smiled back. Even though it was the last thing he felt like doing, he would not ruin their evening.

"I am ready for supper." She grinned.

"Levi grinned back. I am too.

Shall we go?" He offered his hand.

"Jah." She took his hand and he helped her up into the buggy.

Levi went around and stepped up into the driver's seat. He backed out and headed toward town deciding to wait until they were on their way home, to have their discussion. She was so happy about going to supper, he did not want to ruin her evening.

"Levi pulled the buggy up in front of, Zook's Country Cupboard, their favorite restaurant. He stepped out of the buggy to secure Leo to the hitching post. He then went around to help Emmy down.

"Ready to go eat?"Levi asked.

"Jah, I have missed eating here."

"I have too." Levi glanced up

as Sadie the head waitress greeted them.

"Levi, Emily, it has been a long time. It is *gut* to see you. Follow me and I will take you to a table." She smiled.

Once they were seated Sadie gave them menu's and they both ordered the evening special, of pot roast, green beans, mashed potatoes, gravy, homemade bread , and lemonade.

"How are you doing now that you have been home for a couple of weeks?" Emily asked. "Are you happy and are you glad that you are back and working at your *familye's* store?"

Levi heard the uncertainty in her voice as she asked those questions. "Emmy, I am doing well. I am very happy to be home and back working with *mie daadi, daed* and *bruders*. I am here to stay, I do not plan to ever leave again, so you do not need to be concerned. I promised you I was home to stay, *Leibchen, Ich lieb dich* and I meant every word." He smiled.

"That makes me very happy. *Ich lieb dich* too, so much."

"That is *gut* and makes me very happy as well." He smiled. A little while later after they finished their apple pie, Levi asked, "Are you through?"

"*Jah, danke* for the meal, it was very *gut*."She smiled back.

Levi paid their bill and then helped Emily with her coat, before they headed out to his buggy.

Chapter Fourteen

Once they were back in the buggy, Levi headed toward Emily's *farmhaus*. A little ways out of town he pulled the buggy off of the road. He parked it underneath a tree, where they could talk and would have some privacy, in case a car or another buggy were to come by.

"Why are we stopping, Levi?" Emily looked over at him for an answer.

"The other night I told you I had something I wanted to share with you tonight, that happened while I was on *Rumspringa*? *Ich lieb dich* very much, Emmy and I do not want any secrets between us. I want us to always be open and honest with one another."

"Levi, I want you to know you can always *kume* to me no matter what and I will always be open and honest with you. I want you to feel comfortable to share anything with me."

Levi prayed, *please Gott, let her feel the same once she hears mie news*. "Emmy, this is not something I am proud of. I made a decision that I should not have made. I worked with three *menner* at *mie* job and they asked me to move in and share their apartment with them. They had three bedrooms so each of had our own room, which worked out very well. We got along well and it saved all of us money, so that was a *gut* decision. After I had been there a couple of months we were invited to go to a New Years Eve party, put on by our boss's. When my roommates told me I needed to go, I said *nee* at first, but they told me our boss would be offended if we did not attend. I finally gave in and went to the party. When we arrived we were seated at a large round table and introduced to nine other people. On one side of me was one of *mie* buddies and on the other side was a *maedel* named

Macy. Her and two other *maedel's* were from another company and were in town on business. They all seemed very nice. While we were waiting for the party to start a waiter brought around a tray with tall glasses of punch and set one down in front of each of us. As the evening went on our glasses were constantly refilled and there were peanuts and other snacks sitting on the table. Several of the people who had worked at the job and had been there for a few years, were honored for the *gut* job they were doing. The last thing I remember of that night after drinking several glasses of punch was feeling really strange."

"*Ack*, Levi. Was there something in the punch?"

"*Jah,* I found out later that it had Rum in it." Levi heard her gasp in shock. "*Jah*, that was *mie* reaction too, the next day when I was told. I had never had alcohol, so I did not realize that until it was too late and I had drank several glasses throughout the evening.

"What happened, Levi?"

Levi drew in a deep breath and let it out before he said, "I woke up the next morning and could not remember anything after that last glass of punch. I was up stairs in bed in one of the bedrooms and had no idea how I had gotten there. The worst part was I was not alone, Macy was beside me.."

"*Ack, nee*, Levi," She cried!

"Emmy, I am so sorry. We did not either one know how we got there together. We did not remember anything. She said she had never drank alcohol either. We did not know if anything had happened between us, we could not remember anything. I went into the bathroom to take a shower and get dressed, when I came back out she was gone. No one seemed to know her or where she was from. All I knew was she had told me the night before that she was from out of state. We basically talked about me being Amish. She wanted to know all about our lifestyle."

"*Ack*, Levi. Maybe nothing happened between you."

She looked so hopeful that he had not been unfaithful to her. Levi's heart was breaking with the news he had to give her next. "Emmy, I am so sorry. The worst mistake I made was going on *Rumspringa*. I had no idea something like this could happen. If I had not gone, I would never be in this position."

"Levi, I have a feeling there is more, you might as well tell me the rest." She sighed dejectedly.

He felt like such a heel, as the *Englischer's* would say. "I am so sorry, Emmy, unfortunately there is more. When I came out of the barn this morning with *daed* and the *buwes* and we walked into the kitchen, there was an *Englischer maedel* sitting at our kitchen table. She had an infant carrier sitting on the floor beside her."

"*Ack, nee*, Levi, *nee.*" She dropped her head into her hands and began to sob next to him.

"Please Emmy, do not cry. I am so very sorry. I did not do this knowingly. I would never have intentionally been unfaithful to you. You are *mie* life. *Ich Lieb Dich* with *mie* whole heart,

Liebchen. I did not know this *maedel* and I do not remember any part of being with her. I am so very sorry, I pray you can forgive me. When Emily looked up at him with tears running down her face, his heart ached at what he was putting her through.

"You have a child, Levi?" She asked.

And it seemed to Levi there was no feeling in her at that point and it really scared him. "*Jah*, Emmy," he said softly. After looking at her, I know in *mie* heart she is mine. Miss Chambers left with little Katie, that is her name, after taking a sample of what they called DNA from me. She said she had to be sure, but after looking at Katie, I know she is *mie dochder*."

He drew a deep breath and let it out slowly while he waited for her to say something.

"Please take me home, Levi."

"Emmy, please do not leave it like this. *Ich Lieb Dich* so much."

"*Ich Lieb Dich* too, Levi. But right now I do not like you very much. I want to go home, I need time alone to think and pray."

"I will take you home, Emmy."

Levi picked up the reins and moved Leo back out onto the road, heading toward Emmy's *farmhaus*. His heart was breaking, he had never seen Emmy look so defeated and it was his fault. He had done this to her. *Gott, please help me to know what to do.* Levi pulled up in front of Emmy's door and jumped down to go around and help her, He walked her up onto the porch.

"*Danke* for the *gut* meal. *Guder nacht*, Levi." She turned to go into the *haus*.

"Emmy, wait, Please do not leave like this."

" I am sorry, Levi. I do not want to hurt you, but there is nothing more to say. I do not know if I can live with this. I have to have some time and I need to pray."

"I am so sorry, Emmy. I never meant for this to happen. If I was able to change this, I would not go on *Rumspringa*, but I cannot."

"I know you cannot change this, Levi. I am trying to be honest with you too and I do not know what to do. I never even dreamed I would be faced with something like this with you and I am not sure what to do about it. Please give me some time. I do not know what I am going to do."

"I will give you whatever time

you need and I will be praying too, Emmy, *guder nacht.*" He said as she went inside and closed the door.

Chapter Fifteen

Levi headed home. His heart was breaking at what he was putting Emmy through. *Gott please help her. I am so sorry.*

Levi walked into the *haus* after taking care of his horse and the buggy. *Mamm, daed*, Jacob, Joseph and Deborah were sitting in the front room. Everyone else were already upstairs in bed for the *nacht.*

"From the expression on your face I think it did not go well with Emily," *Mamm* said."

"*Nee*, it did not." She is devastated as I feared she would be." Levi shook his head. "I cannot help her in this, she has to make the decision on whether she can forgive me and live with this. I pray she can, but only *Gott* knows."

"*Sohn*, I know you are hurting and Emily is also. We are praying and *Gott* will work this out. If Emily *liebs* you the way I believe she does, she will be able to accept it and *kume* to you to work it out. We will continue to pray." *Mamm* hugged him.

:We are praying too, Levi. Deborah offered and his *bruders* agreed they were also praying.

"*Danke*, I appreciate your prayers and support."

"It is getting late, we all need to head upstairs to bed. Try to get some rest, *Sohn*."*Daed* and *mamm* stood and they all headed upstairs. When he and the twins closed the door Jacob said, " Emily will *kume* to you. She *liebs* you, she is hurting right now, in time she will make the right decision, you were meant to be together." Jacob laid his hand on Levi's shoulder. "Try to get some rest you look so tired."

"Jacob is right, Levi and we are all praying." Joseph agreed.

"*Danki, bruders*. That means a lot to me. I appreciate your support. I made a very bad choice in going on *Rumspringa.* Even though I do not remember anything about that night, it does not change the fact that it happened. If I had it to do over, I would never have gone. Please learn by my bad choice and do not go on *Rumspringa*, please."

"I never planned to go," Jacob said as he climbed into bed.

"I have changed *mie* mind, I was planning on it, but after this I have decided not to." Joseph told them as he climbed into his bed that sat next Jacob's.

"That is *gut.* I am glad you have both learned from *mie* mistake and have made this decision. I would not wish this heartache on either of you." Levi climbed under the quilts in his bed that was across the room from these two *bruders,* whom he *liebed* so much.

"*Guder nacht, buwes.*"

"*Guder nacht,.*" *bruder*, they chorused.

******

When Emily walked into the kitchen, *mamm* was the only one still up and she was sitting at the table. Emily sat in the chair next to her.

"*Liebchen* what has happened? You were so happy when you left and now you have obviously been crying."

"*Ack, Mamm.* I do not know what to do." Emmy started to sob again, her heart was breaking.

"Do not cry so, *Liewi*. Tell me what has happened and I will try to help you sort it out."

In between sobs Emily finally managed to explain what Levi had told her. "*Mie* heart is breaking, *Mamm*. I never dreamed I would ever have to face Levi being unfaithful to me."

"Emily, I can understand you feel betrayed, *Liebchen*, but if this happened the way you just told me, he was not knowingly unfaithful. If you are honest with yourself, do you believe he would have allowed this to happen had he been aware of what he was doing?"

Emily looked at her *mamm* and then closed her eyes for a moment. When she opened them she said, " *Nee, Mamm,* if I am honest I know in *mie* heart he would not, but it still happened and I am having a hard time dealing with it."

"I can understand how you feel, *Liewi,* but *y*ou have a decision to make. You must decide if you *lieb* him enough to not only forgive him, but also be able to put this behind you and help him raise his *boppli dochder* as your own. You must consider how devastated you were the year he was away from you. You basically placed your life on hold until he returned. I do not want to see you do that to yourself again. *Liebchen.* You need to spend some time in thought and prayer. *Gott* will lead you in this decision."

"Danke, Mamm for always being here for me."

"Ack, you are *mie dochder* and *Ich lieb dich.* You can always *kume* to me."

"I have never doubted that, you always have been here for me and *Ich lieb dich* for it."

"You are tired, it is late,

Liebchen and you need to be in bed. Morning *kumes* early. Try to get some rest and know that me and your *daed* are praying."

Emily hugged her *mamm* and they went upstairs to bed.

Chapter Sixteen

It had been a very long week and Levi was tired as he helped his *daed* and *bruders* close the store. He had not been sleeping well. He had hoped to see Emily but evidently she had been avoiding running into him all week. He usually saw her as they got to work each morning, but she evidently went in early to avoid seeing him. Not that he could blame her. She said she needed some time and as much as he missed her he would give her the time she needed and pray they would still be able to have a future together.

Once the store was closed, Levi walked out with his *daed* and *bruders*. He climbed into his buggy and headed home. When he pulled up the driveway toward the barn he noticed Miss Chambers car parked across from the *haus*. He took care of his horse and headed into the inside. As he went into the kitchen he greeted her, his *mamm* and two *schweschders*.

"Hello, Levi. Please sit down and I will go over this information with you." Miss Chambers told him.

Levi couldn't help but notice the smile on *mamm's* face as she held Katie in her lap. He pulled the chair out across from Miss Chambers and sat down so he could listen to what she had to say.

"The DNA test came back showing you are Katie's biological father, Levi. I have the paperwork for you to fill out and sign in order for you to take full legal custody of Katie."

"I will sign your papers. Katie is mine and I will take full responsibility for her. I will love her and raise her to the best of *mie* ability. She will be raised in church and in a loving home with a *familye* who loves her as well." He promised.

"That is good. I know her

mother would be pleased. That is what she wanted for her daughter." Miss Chambers gave the paperwork to Levi.

He took a pen, filled it out and then signed it before returning it back to her.

"Thank you, if you have any questions, I will be at the hotel in town until about eleven in the morning. There are enough diapers and formula in the diaper bag for a week. I need to go." She went over to Katie and placed a kiss on her forehead. "I will miss you sweet Katie, but I feel I am leaving you in good hands."

Levi noticed the tears well up in her eyes. We will take *gut* care of her."

"Thank you, Levi. I am sure you will. Good day." She said as she went out to get into her car.

She waved as she backed out of the driveway and onto the road, to head back toward town.

When Levi came back into the kitchen, *mamm* handed Katie to him so she could finish putting supper on the table. He could not help but smile as he looked at his tiny *dochder*. Even under the circumstances she was a precious gift from *Gott,* and he already *liebed* her.

After supper was over *daed* said, "Deborah, Maryanne, please *redd up* the kitchen, *mamm* and I want to talk to Levi in the front room for a few minutes."

Levi wondered what his parents wanted to talk to him about. He sat on the sofa with Katie in his lap.

"*Sohn, Mamm* and I have been waiting for you to return to give this to you."

Levi glanced up from Katie to ask what his *daed* was saying, but before he could his *daed* continued.

"Great *Aenti* Elizabeth left her property and *haus* to you, *Sohn*. You were her oldest Nephew and she *liebed you.* Since she never married or had *kinner* of her own, she wanted her property and *haus* to go to you. We have taken care of it while you have been gone. We painted the outside of the *haus* and barn two months ago. The inside needs to be painted and your *bruders* and I will help you paint it when you are ready. It is furnished but you may want to change some things." *Daed* looked at him.

"I do not know what to say, this is a very generous gift, *Daed*."

Levi was surprised by this because usually the youngest child inherited, but in this case his youngest *bruder* would inherit his parents property, when they moved into the *dawdi haus.* Evidently that is why his Great Aenti, was able to leave her *haus* and property to him. This was an amazing gift. *Danke Gott,* for this blessing. "*Daed, Mamm*, this is a *wunderbaar* gift. I liebed *Aenti* Elizabeth and enjoyed helping her, I was sad when I received your letter telling me she had gone to be with *Gott*. She was a special person."

"*Jah*, she was, *Sohn* and we all miss her, but we know she is with *Gott* now."

"*Danke Daed, Mamm.* I appreciate this and I so appreciate *Aenti* Elizabeth giving this gift to me. I wish there was some way I could say *danke* to her too."

"The best way you can say *danke* to her, is to enjoy the *haus* and land and to be happy there." *Daed* stood and laid his hand on Levi's shoulder. Now it is time we were all in bed. The *buwes* and I moved the crib down from the attic for Katie, into the extra bedroom and moved your bed, dresser and chair, in with her bed. She has been changed and fed, her bottles are in the refrigerator for when she awakes in the night for one. Her diapers are in the diaper bag in your room as well. If you need me in the night *kume* get me." *Mamm* smiled and they went upstairs. His *schweschders* and *bruders* had already gone up without interrupting his discussion with *mamm* and *daed*. Levi took

Katie and went up to his room. This would be an interesting night he was sure. He had never changed a diaper, but he would figure it out, Katie was his *dochder,* he already *liebed* her and he would manage to take care of her.

Levi heard a noise and glanced at the clock on his bedside table, it said 2 o'clock. You've got to be kidding, he had forgotten *boppli's* were awake at this time of the morning. He stumbled out of bed in his pajamas and started out of the room. He stubbed his toe on the leg of the bed on his way out. "Ouch!" He cried and hopped half way down the hall on one foot, holding his other one in his hand, as he finally made his way down the stairs to warm a bottle. He'd nearly broken his little toe and the way it felt right now, he was convinced he'd surely be crippled for life.

By the time he reached the crib his *daed* and *bruders* had brought down from the attic earlier, his *dochder* was in a real temper. He picked her up hoping to sooth her. One whiff had him wrinkling his nose, oh man, what was that disgusting smell? Levi carefully lifted the edge of Katie's diaper. He took a peek, what in the world was that? it looked just like mustard, but it certainly didn't smell like any mustard he's ever seen. "Whew little one, we are definitely going to have to do something about that. But what he was not sure, he did not have a clue on how to change a *boppli*. *Gott, I'm definitely going to need some assistance here.* Levi had no sooner finished that statement when he noticed something that suspiciously resembled the gooey mustard stuff oozing through the leg of the gown the baby had on. Levi lifted the baby's foot and immediately regretted the gesture. She was soaked in the stuff clear to her neck. "Oh man, how can someone so small create such an odor? His tiny *dochder* started to scream louder if that was possible. He had to do something; she was going to wake up the whole *haus*. He thought about Emmy, she would know what to do. He shook his head what in the world are you thinking? Get your mind back on the business at hand. You are definitely in a fix here!

"Levi, *mamm* came in the door.

"*Ack, Mamm.* I am sorry the *boppli* awakened you, but am I ever glad to see you. Little Katie needs a new diaper and I'm afraid she is going to have to have clean clothes too. She is all soaked and this stuff looks just like mustard! Is it supposed to look like that? His forehead creased in concern. Whew the way she smells I think she's gonna need a bath too."

Mamm chuckled, "All newborns look like that the first several diapers. I will give you instructions, but It's time you learned so you will know how."

Levi looked at her and he knew she was right. Katie was his responsibility and he needed to know how to take care of her. "I know I need to learn and I will, but can you do it this time and I'll watch so I can learn? I don't even know where to start." He stood there for a moment.

"*Nee*, but I'll tell you what to do." *Mamm* smiled sympathetically.

Levi looked down at the mess the baby was in and back over at her. Well, he might as well get started, he swallowed and then laid a blanket underneath the baby and pulled her sleeper off of her. "Oh man! How can such a tiny little thing smell so bad?" Whew, we're going to have to air out the room *kind* when we get you all cleaned up so we can stand to stay in here."

Mamm smiled. "*Jah*, the odor is pretty strong, but it is too cold to open the window. You will need to leave the door open when you are through."

By the time Levi was through bathing Katie, redressing her and changing the sheets, he was exhausted and ready to go back to bed.

"*Danke,* for your directions *Mamm.* I will know what to do if this happens again. I appreciate it. Go back to bed and try to get a little more rest while I feed Katie.

"You did *gut, Sohn.*" She smiled. "I will see you in the morning."

Levi sat down and fed his little *dochder* a bottle. He had to smile to himself, she had caused a ruckus for sure and certain, the whole *haus* had been in here to see what was happening while he was taking care of her. *Mamm* had reassured them and sent them all back to bed. Katie finished her bottle and was now sound to sleep, so Levi climbed back under the quilts. It had been quite a *nacht,* he sighed. In just a few minutes

Levi was also back to sleep.

Chapter Seventeen

Emily came downstairs the next morning, she was looking forward to the auction in spite of all that was happening between her and Levi. "*Guder Mariye,*

Mamm What can I help you with?"

"*Guder Mariye, Liewi.* You may set the table and then Sit down. Your *daed* and the *kinner* will be in any moment. We will have breakfast and then load everything into the wagon and head to auction."

Mamm finished placing the food on the table while Emily set it for the meal. Just as she finished the family came in the door of the kitchen and took a seat ready to eat.

"Are you feeling up to going to the auction, *dochder.*" *Daed* asked. Emily smiled at him. He was such a caring *daed.* "*Jah*, I am looking forward to going."

"That is *gut.* As soon as we are finished with breakfast *buwes,* we need to load the wagon for the auction." *Daed told them.*

"All right, *Daed. W*e are almost finished and we will be ready to help," John said and continued eating.

Emily grinned when Steven nodded since he had his mouth full. He always seemed to be starving. He was definitely a growing *buwe.* For the next few minutes it was quiet around the table, while everyone finished their meal, so they could get started to the auction. Once they finished eating, Emily asked, "*Mamm* is there anything I can help you with now that the kitchen is *redd up?*"

"You can help me put the jars of jam in those boxes." She indicated the ones stacked up on the floor against the wall."

Emily picked up the boxes and

started loading the jars of jam into them.

"It looks like you can use some help."Nancy, Brenda and Susan stepped up beside Emily and started putting jam into the box along with her. In no time they had all of the jars finished. John and Steven came in just as they were done.

"Ready for us to load the boxes?" John asked.

"*Jah, danke,* " Emily answered as Nancy, Brenda and Susan started placing the plates of cookies, cinnamon rolls, pastries and the rest of the items in the boxes they would sell at the auction later that morning. All of the boxes were soon ready for the *buwes* to load.

"I will be out in just a few minutes. I need to go to the

restroom." Emily said and rushed up the stairs. She headed back downstairs and just as she reached the bottom, Nancy said, "*Ack* Emily, I was just *kuming* to see if you are ready."

"*Jah*, I am, I hope I did not hold everyone up."

"*Nee, Daed* went to the barn to get the tarp for the wagon. I look forward to Auction day. I am so glad they were able to clear the tree that fell across the road to the Auction grounds, so we could take the wagons and buggy. Otherwise we would not have been able to go this time" She grinned.

"*Ack, Jah*. That is *gut*. I always enjoy it too." Emily smiled at her *schweschder's* excitement.

"Ack, looks like *Daed*, John and Steven have the tarp on the wagons and they are ready to go,

Nancy told her.

Emily climbed in after Nancy and sat next to her in the buggy. When they were all seated *daed* backed out of the driveway and headed for the auction.

A few minutes later, *daed* pulled in and parked the buggy behind where they would set up their booths and tables. Emily started to step down from the buggy and realized John was standing there, he offered her a hand down.

"*Danke, bruder.*

"*Welkom*," he smiled.

Jacob walked up just after Nancy stepped down.

"Looks like you and your *familye* are all set up and ready for the day." She said.

"*Jah*, we are, so I thought I would *kume* to help all of you set up." Jacob offered.

"That is very thoughtful of you, Jacob." Faith smiled. "We will certainly welcome the help." They were quite suddenly interrupted. When a *boppli* started to cry.

Emily glanced over at the table where Levi and Jacob's *familye* were sitting. She realized when Levi placed a small *boppli* on his shoulder and began to pat her tiny back, that it was his *dochder*. The DNA test he had been waiting for had obviously *kume* back, proving the *boppli* was in fact his *dochder*. Emily's heart ached, she turned away and tried to stay busy unloading the boxes and sitting the jam and baked goods on the table for the auction, Nancy, Brenda and Susan jumped in to help Emily and *mamm* get ready, the auction would start soon and they needed to be organized.

Daed and the *buwes* set more boxes on one of the tables for the *maedels* to unload and went back to the buggies to get some more.

Emily noticed how Nancy's eyes lit up each time Jacob joined them, adding boxes for them to unload. Jacob was a *gut mann* and he would make Nancy a *gut* husband. Emily prayed he just would not follow his *bruder's* choice and go on *Rumspringa*. Emily would not wish this heartache on any of her *schweschders*."

Chapter Eighteen

As the day drug by for Emily, she tried to occupy herself with customers at their table, but she could not keep from glancing over at the Graber table. She noticed Nancy was there with Jacob and she was holding Levi's *boppli.*

Before Emily could even think about how she felt about that, Nancy and Jacob came back to their table holding the *boppli*. She handed her to *mamm*. Emily could not believe her *schweschder* would bring Levi's *boppli* to their table, knowing how Emily felt about the whole situation. Then she felt guilty, she knew it was not the *boppli's* fault this happened and she needed someone to love and care for her. Emily tried to ignore them and waited on a customer. She had just taken the money and added it to the cash box, when she heard *mamm* say, A*ck* she is a *shee boppli*."

"*Jah*, she is, *Mamm*. Emily do you want to see her?" Nancy asked,

"*Nee,* I am going to go over to the barn and see how the quilts are doing. I will be back in a little while." As she left she heard Nancy say, "I probably should not have brought the *boppli* here. I did not mean to hurt Emily." She did not hear *mamm's* response she was too far away by then. Emily's heart was breaking, she *liebed* Levi, but she felt betrayed by him.

******

Levi could not help but see and hear Emily's response to his *dochder*. His heart was breaking, he knew he had hurt her, but Katie was his responsibility and he prayed in time maybe Emmy would be able to forgive him and accept that he has a kind, that just maybe she would be able to *lieb* her and want to still have a future with him. Please *Gott* I pray it will be so.

"Levi, I am going over to the

Quilt barn to see how the sale is going do you want a break and go with me?" Deborah asked.

Levi looked up at his *schweschder*. "*Jah*, I would, *danke*."

"Levi, I will take care of Katie while you are gone if you want me to." Maryann offered.

"*Danke*, Maryann. We will not be gone long." Levi handed his *dochder* to his youngest *schweschder*. He was sure she could handle her, but *mamm* was here too in case she needed something.

Levi and Deborah walked over to the quilt auction barn and went inside. The quilt that was being auctioned was hung up on a clothes line and Levi knew by looking at it that it was one of Emmy's. She was an exceptional quilter and her quilts always sold well. He saw her over by the table talking to her two younger *bruders*, Steven and Micah. They were taking care of their table with the quilts to be auctioned off. The proceeds from the quilt sale would all go into the community fund, which would be available to help any *familye* in their district if they needed it.

Levi saw Emmy leave the barn and he wondered if she left because she saw him *kume* in, he hoped not, but suspected it was so. *Please Gott help her.*

******

Emily left when she saw Levi and Deborah *kume* into the auction barn, it was not in her to be rude and she did not want to have to talk to him. As she slipped out the side door and made her way back she prayed, *Please Gott help me, I lieb Levi so much. But I am so hurt over him betraying me. What am I supposed to do? Please help me to make the right decision about him and his boppli. I do not know if I can lieb and raise this woman's boppli, that Levi was unfaithful with.* As Emily approached the Graber table, which she had to walk by to get to theirs, she heard Levi's *boppli* crying. She tried to ignore it, but couldn't help but glance that way. She could see that Levi's *mamm* was tied up with a customer and Maryann, Levi's youngest *schweschder,* was trying to quiet the *boppli* by patting her tiny back, but she was not having much success. Emily noticed they were the only two there. Emily tried to ignore them and walk on by, but she could see the distress on Maryann's face as the *boppli* continued to cry. She sighed and finally went over to see if she could help her.

"Maryann, how can I help? Emily asked.

"I changed her diaper, but I think she is hungry. I do not know how to heat her a bottle and *mamm* is with a customer."

Emily could see Maryann was about to cry along with the *boppli*. She felt for her.

" Where are her bottles?" Emily asked.

Maryann took one out of the small chest it was in with ice and handed it to Emily. "I do not know how to warn it and she cannot drink it cold."

"Nee, you are correct. I will take it over to the restroom and warm it under the water faucet. I will be back in a few minutes."Emily told her. Emily took it over to the restroom and once she had ran the hot water over the bottle for a few minutes, it broke the chill and began to warm the formula. She took it back over to the Graber table where Maryann was walking back and forth with the *boppli.* Little Katie was red in the face from crying and Maryann was wiping her tiny nose. Emily noticed Karen was involved with another customer. There was a chair there so Emily said, "do you want me to take her?"

Maryann did not hesitate she handed Emily the *boppli.*

"*Danki,* Emily. I feel so bad, but I could not do anything to sooth her."

"It was not your fault *Leibchen*, she is hungry and only a bottle is going to help right now."

Emily sat down with the *boppli* and gave her the warm bottle. She looked down at her and noticed she looked just like Levi. Her eyes were already turning green and what little hair she had was the color of wheat, just like his, his *daed's* and his siblings. *Mamm* was correct when she said she was a shee *boppli* and as much as Emily did not want to, she could not help but smile at her. She was precious. So sweet. She looked up at Emily as she hungrily sucked her bottle. When her tiny hand wrapped around Emily's finger she was lost. How could she not *lieb* this precious *boppli* when she *liebed* her *daed* so much? Okay, *Gott*, I guess I have *mie* answer to *mie* prayers. I can *lieb* her, even under the circumstances. Emily glanced up and realized Levi was standing next to her.

"Emily?"

"Hello, Levi." She was hungry and Maryann did not know how to warm her bottle. Your *mamm* was tied up with a customer. I heard her crying so I stopped to help."

"*Danki*, I appreciate it."

Katie handed the *boppli* to Levi. She was not ready to give her up, but knew she must go back to help her *mamm*. "I must go." She said and started to walk away.

"Emmy, *danke* for helping Maryann with Katie."

"*Welkom,* Levi." She walked back over to her *familye's* table. Nancy smiled at her, She had obviously seen Emily holding the *boppli* and talking to Levi. "We need to help *mamm* box up the rest of the items so we will be ready to go home."Emily did not mention Levi or the *boppli*. She was not ready to talk about them.

Chapter Nineteen

Levi had watched Katie with his little *maedel* and the way her eyes softened when she looked at Katie. He prayed maybe there was still hope for them. He helped his *familye* box up the few items that they had left. It had been a productive day, but everyone was tired and ready to go home.

"*Kinner*, we have been invited to join The Mast *Familye* at Amos and Barbara's for Thanksgiving. Is that going to create a hardship for you Levi?"

"*Nee, mamm.* I am praying Emily and I will have worked things out before then, but if not we are adults and we will manage."

"Levi, *daed* walked into the *haus* after they arrived home and had everything put away in its place. I have some time right now if you want to go over to your *haus* with me. You can decide what you want to keep and what you want to replace."

"I will keep Katie for you,

Deborah offered.

"*Danke*, Deborah. I appreciate that. He handed his tiny *boppli* over to his *schweschder*. Levi took his coat back off of the rack, along with his hat and followed *daed* across to his new *haus*. The property resided between *mamm and daed's property* and *daadi* and *maami* Graber's property. They walked into the *haus* and Levi glanced around. He had always *liebed* this *haus*. This is a nice *haus Daed*. I am blessed that *Aenti* left it to me."

"*Jah*, it is *Sohn*, and she wanted you to have it. She prayed everyday that you would return so you could accept it. She *liebed* you."

"I *liebed* her too and I so appreciate this *wunderbaar* gift." Levi said and followed his *daed* upstairs. There were four bedrooms on the second floor as well as one on the ground floor and a fully stocked quilt room. Emily would *lieb* this. Levi thought, if she ever lived here. His thought took some of the excitement out of this for Levi .

"Well, *Sohn*, what do you want to replace and what shades do you want to paint inside?"

"Can I take a little time to think about it, *Daed*?"

"Of course. Since Thanksgiving is next week. Why do we not plan to start working on the *haus* the Monday after?"

"That will be *gut, Daed, danki.*"

"*Welkom.* We should go over to our barn now, it is time to milk."

******

Emily helped *Mamm* and the *maedels* fix supper that evening but she could not keep her mind off of Levi and little Katie. Could she put this behind her and make a future with Levi?

"Emily are you here with us *kind*?"

"I am sorry, *Mamm*. I was woolgathering What did you say?"

"*Mammi* and *daadi* have invited us to have the Thanksgiving meal with them and they have invited the Graber *familye* to join us. Is that going to be hard for you?"

Emily swallowed before she answered. "*Nee, Mamm* I will make it work." Emily knew she had to make a decision here. Her feelings were effecting not only her *familye,* but also Levi's and

their *familyes* had been very close
frienden since she and Levi were
bopplin. That night Emily did not
get very much sleep, she spent
most of the night awake in prayer.
When she got to work that
morning, Rebekah met her.

"Emily, you have dark circles
underneath your eyes. What is
keeping you awake? Is it what is
going on between you and Levi?
Unless you tell me differently, I
am thinking it is."

"*Jah,* Rebekah." Katie shared
with her *frienden,* all that had
taken place, since she saw her and
about holding and feeding Little
Katie at the auction.

"I thought so. When I talked
with you briefly in the auction
barn while we were sorting our
quilts, you were not yourself then.
I know that holding Levi's *boppli*

on the way back to your table must have been hard for you."

"It was hard, Rebekah. She is such a sweet *boppli*. I have a decision to make. This situation between me and Levi is effecting both of our *familye's* not just us.

"*Jah*, I can see that it is. When we have a close *familye* like we both have, anything that hurts us effects our *lieb* ones too."

"*Jah*, it does and I am the one who has to make this decision. Levi made a bad choice that placed us all in this situation, but he cannot change that now and he has no choice, he has to take care of his *boppli*. I understand that. I would not *lieb* him like I do, if he was a *mann* who did not own up to his responsibilities. I have forgiven him, but I am having a hard time getting past the hurt it has caused me. "

"I can understand that, Emily, but you must remember even though he made the mistake, he is hurting too. You must decide if you *lieb* him enough to put this behind you, so you can help him raise his *boppli dochder* and make a future with him. If you do not then you must let him go so he can find someone else who will and you can both go forward with your future. I tell you this because *Ich lieb dich* and I want you to be happy." Rebekah gave her a hug.

"I know you do and I cannot argue with you because I know you are correct and I appreciate it."

On a brighter subject, what happened between you and Elijah Yoder, Sunday evening after we left? I could see the way you looked at each other?"

Rebekah blushed and Emily grinned. *Ack*, so that is the way it is. How long has this been going on? I cannot believe you did not tell me." Emily frowned at her *frienden*.

"We have not been seeing each other, or I would have. He came in the other *nacht* when our *familye* was having supper at the Country our Cupboard. He walked over to speak to us. I had not seen him since shortly before Levi left. He said he had been helping his Uncle in another district and had just returned. *Mamm* and *daed* invited him to sit with us, since he was alone and we got to talking. I found I really liked him and he seemed to like me to. I haven't seen him since then until he sat across from me at the singing.

He asked me to go for a buggy ride this Saturday and I find I am looking forward to it." She grinned.

"The Bishop's *Sohn*, Rebekah? Well, that should be interesting. I am happy for you. If he makes you happy, that's all that is important to me, *mie frienden*. I will look forward to hearing all about it next week. We better get back to work." She grinned.

Emily thought all the rest of the day about what Rebekah said. Just before they were to close for the day, Ellen Beiler's *mamm* came in and bought a dozen cupcakes. She nodded to Emily and Rebekah as she left. Emily had the thought that, Ellen would probably be the first in line to step into Emily's place, if she left Levi. The thought nearly crushed her.

"I know what you are thinking, but you cannot let Ellen Beiler's attraction to Levi, sway your decision.' Rebekah whispered next to Emily."

Emily gave her *frienden* a shaky smile.

When *maami* came up front and turned the closed sign, then pulled the curtain over the door, Emily was ready to go home. She knew she needed to talk to Levi and she would not allow Ellen Beiler's attraction to him, to influence Emily's decision.

"It is time to go home *maedels,* it has been a busy day."

"*Guder nacht*, Abigail. I will see you tomorrow." Rebekah slipped into her coat.

"*Guder nacht, mammi.*" Emily hugged her and slipped into his coat as well. She followed

Rebekah out to the barn. After they secured their horses to their buggies. Emily said, " I will think about what you said, be careful going home, Rebekah and I will see you in the morning."

"I will, you be careful too. I will be praying for you and wait to see what you decide to do."

After Rebekah left, Emily prayed for a moment and decided to walk across the street to the Graber Furniture Store. She went inside and was greeted by John.

"Hello, Emily how can I help you?" John asked.

" Hello, John. Is Levi still here?"

"*Jah*, he is. Please have a seat and I will go tell him you are here."

Emily only waited a couple of minutes until Levi walked through the door to the front where she was sitting.

"Emmy, are you all right?"

"*Jah*, I am. Levi. Do you have a little time where we can go somewhere and talk?" She looked up at this *mann* she *liebed* so much. Ellen or no Ellen she could not walk away from Levi and Little Katie. She *liebed* them both..

"*Jah.*" He smiled. I will tell *daed*, I will not be home for a while, so *mamm* will not worry."

******

Levi went through the door and then he was back in just a few minutes. Emily stood up and they went out to Emily's buggy since Levi and the *buwes* had ridden in with their *daed.* "Would you drive?"

"*Jah*, Levi helped Emily up

into the buggy and went around to climb into the driver's seat. He picked up the reins to Emmy's mare and was trying not to get his hopes up, but his heart was pounding. What did Emmy want to talk about? he prayed it was their future together. He found a secluded place to pull off of the road, where they could talk privately. He turned to look at Emmy and waited quietly, for her to tell him why she wanted this time to talk.

******

"Emmy turned toward Levi and said, I appreciate you giving me the time I needed to think and pray." She swallowed before she could continue. "I have had a very hard time dealing with the fact that you were unfaithful to me, even though I realize you do not remember it. I have spent considerable time in prayer about this. I believe that had you been aware, you would never have done this. I also believe you will always be faithful to me in the future. In view of that, I will forgive you for this and after holding little Katie, I realized that I can *lieb* her as *mie* own, because she is part of you and *Ich lieb dich* with all *mie* heart. Levi, I want us to have a future together. I have been so miserable these last several days without you." She began to sob and Levi pulled her into his arms.

"*Ack*, Emmy please do not cry. I wish I could go back and change this, but I cannot. I am so sorry this happened. I promise you I will never do anything to hurt you again. I am so glad you have forgiven me and have *kume* to me tonight. I have missed you and *Ich lieb dich* too, *Liebchen*. Can I pick you up tomorrow after work? I have a surprise I would like to show you?"

"A surprise?"

******

Levi *liebed* the way Emmy's blue eyes lit up at the thought of a surprise. He smiled and said, *Jah*. He hugged her.

"I would *lieb* that, I will be ready." She assured him and grinned through her tears that he gently wiped away.

"*Gut*." Levi picked up the reins and pulled the buggy out onto the road to head to her *haus*. He would walk from her *haus* to his, it was not that far after he took her home.

I can drive the buggy from your *haus* to mine, that way you do not have to walk home." Emily offered.

"*Danke*, but *nee*. It is turning colder out, we may get some snow soon and you need to be inside where it is warm. I will walk, it is not that far. A few minutes later, Levi pulled into the driveway and headed to the barn. He helped Emmy unhitch her buggy and took care of her mare.

"Do you want to see the puppies before you go, they are so cute.?" She grinned up at him.

"Sure, how old are they now?"

"They are nine weeks. They will be old enough to sell in another week. Emily picked up one of the little German Shepherds. This one is *mie* favorite. He is so precious. I *lieb* him. But *daed* will not let us keep one. He breeds them to sell for extra income for the *familye*, but he does not want one. I hope whoever buys him, gives him a *gut* home." She smiled and rubbed his soft fur against her cheek.

"He is cute, that is for sure and certain. He has a pretty face. I am sure your *daed* will find *gut* homes for all of the pups. Generally people do not buy a pup unless they want one. It is a little different than getting one with no cost involved," He smiled."

"I sure you are right." Emily hugged the little pup one more time and then reluctantly set him back in the pen, with his *mamm* and siblings. *Danki,* Levi. I appreciate you unhitching *mie* buggy and taking care of Ruby."

"*Welkom.*" He walked her back to the *haus* and they stepped up onto the back porch and drew her into his arms. He kissed her and was relieved they were back together, he had missed her so much. "*Guder nacht*, Emmy. I will see you tomorrow. *Ich lieb dich*.

"*Guder nacht*, Levi. *Ich lieb dich* too. Just as Emily started to go in the door they heard a buggy pull into the driveway. It was Jacob bringing Nancy home. "*Ack, gut*. Jacob can give you a ride home, so you do not have to walk in the cold." Emmy smiled.

""Sounds like we got here at the right time." Jacob grinned. Need a ride home, bug *bruder*?"

"Levi grinned back. That would be *gut*, little *bruder*. I would appreciate it."

Levi and Jacob saw the *maedels* inside and then headed home.

Chapter Twenty

The next morning Levi and Katie joined them for breakfast. During the meal, Emmy, *mamm* and the *maedels* took turns holding the *boppli.*

"*Daed,* Emily pushed away

her empty plate. "Levi would like to take me to see a *haus*. Could *John*, go with us?"

Before John had a chance to answer, Noah said, "That will be *gut* and your *bruder can go* along. Steven, Micah and I can handle the Buggy store until you get there."

John finished his last bite of breakfast and stood. "I'm ready." He grinned.

******

"*Danki*, we won't be gone long." Levi opened the door for Emmy and John before he followed them out. Once they were settled in the buggy, Levi handed Katie to Emmy. He went around, climbed in and backed the buggy out of the driveway. He headed to their *haus* which was just down the road from the

Graber farm. Only moments later he pulled into the driveway and stopped by the front steps. This is our *haus*. Emmy." Levi smiled.

"*Ack*, Levi, this was your Aenti's *haus*." Wonder brightened her eyes. "How can I ever say *danki* enough? I *lieb* this *haus*. it looks *wunderbaar* for sure and certain. It has been so long since I was here, I cannot wait to see the inside." She grinned as he took Katie and helped her down.

"Your living here with me is all of the thanks I want." He smiled and hugged her. "I have something for you inside."

When they went in the door Levi took Emmy into the front room. He *liebed* the way her bright blue eyes shone as she looked at the rocking chair he'd made for her.

"*Ack*, Levi, it is *wunderbaar*. I can't wait to rock Katie in it." Emily hugged him, he handed her the boppli and she sat in her new chair rocking Katie. Levi and John sat on the sofa across from them while they rocked.

"Sit still and I'll be right back." Levi disappeared into another room and in a minute he was back.

Emmy looked up at him as he came back into the room, joy written all over her face."*Ack,* Levi. *Danki.* Emily handed Katie to Levi and took the tiny puppy from him. She grinned and rubbed the puppy's fur against her cheek. "Mie puppy, He is so soft. Levi, I do not know what to say." Emily choked up.

"You don't need to say anything. You *liebed* this pup and I have been wanting to get a

German Shepherd. When you showed the litter to me when I helped you take care of your horse and buggy last night, I could see you *liebed* this one. I bought him from your *daed* this morning while I was out in the barn with him and your *bruders,* when they were milking. Micah ran him over here for me, before he came in for breakfast." Levi was pleased that Emmy enjoyed sitting in her rocking chair, with Katie and then with the ittle puppy in her lap. It made him feel *gut* that she liked his gifts.

"You're *familye* has taken *gut* care of this place, Levi.

"*Jah*, they have. I could not believe it when *daed* and *mamm* told me *mie* Great-*Aenti* Elizabeth had left it to me and that they had cared for it for the last ten months, since she went to be with Gott. It is a *wunderbaar* gift, for sure and certain. We are going to paint it inside next week, but I wanted you to choose the shades you want the walls to be, Emmy and I will replace any furniture you want me to."

"*Danke,* Levi." Emmy stood up and smiled at him.

"*Ich lieb dish mie*, Emmy." Levi kissed the top of her head, resisting the kiss he wanted to share with her—but certainly not in front of John--her *bruder and his frienden.*

John cleared his throat. "We better go through the rest of the *haus*, so we can get headed to work soon."

"*Jah*, Levi placed the pup in his kennel and followed John and Emmy, carrying Katie, up the stairs. He showed them the furnishings in the three bedrooms. One for Katie, along with their future *kinner* and the master bedroom which were all furnished. He noticed that Emmy realized about the same time he did that there was a single bed in the master bedroom. I will change that before we get married." Levi told her and smiled when her face turned bright red.

"Danki, Levi. I am happy to see there are four bedrooms up here, that is *wunderbaar*. Your *familye* made this furniture did you not?"

"*Jah, mie daed* made most of it.

"It's *wunderbaar!* I've never seen any furniture more beautiful. The light oak is just what I would have chosen. I *lieb* it all. The only thing I would change is the colors of the walls."

"I have to agree with her, Levi, this is a very nice *haus*." John said. *Ack,* by the way, I couldn't be happier that you are going to one day soon be *mie bruder*-in-law."

"*Danki*, John. That means a lot coming from you. Let us go back downstairs and I will show you the other two rooms."

They looked at the downstairs bedroom, which was furnished the same as the ones upstairs, with just a different quilt on the bed. When they reached the next room, Emmy gasped. " a quilt room. I had forgotten about your *Aenti's lieb* for quilting. I was in this room one time many years ago. Ack, Levi. It is *wunderbaar.* I cannot believe she left it stocked with material and everything I could possibly need to quilt." Emmy ran her hand over the quilt rack. I have always wanted a rack of *mie* own. I always shared *mamm's.*" She gave him a bright smile."I *lieb* this *haus*, the puppy, rocking chair and everything in it. I cannot wait to live in it with you." she whispered softly.

"That is *gut*. I want you to be happy, always." Levi smiled down at her and kissed her forehead. "We had better go, so John and I can get to work."

They headed back to Emily and John's to drop them off. It was supposed to snow tonight, so Levi asked Emmy to go on a sleigh ride and to supper with him the next evening and she agreed.

Micah had agreed to go over after *schul* to let the pup out on his way home each afternoon.

Levi stopped by his *haus* to drop Katie off to Mamm, she had offered to watch her while Levi was working and then he headed to work at his *familye's* furniture store. He was very pleased that Emmy liked the *haus,* the furniture and the puppy. He was looking forward to their evening together tomorrow.

When Levi walked into the store his *daed* looked up and asked, How did Emily like the house, *Sohn."*

"She *liebed* it. I asked her what colors she wanted us to paint each room. She wrote then down for me, I have the list, so we can go ahead and start painting next week." Levi answered as he followed Jacob out to load the desk they were going to deliver.

******

The next day drug by for Emily, she was excited about going on a sleigh ride with Levi and she could hardly wait. It had snowed as Levi had said it was supposed to, so they could go on the sleigh."

"Emily, if you want to go up and get ready for your sleigh ride with Levi, we are through here, *Leibchen*."

"Danke, Mamm. Emily did not hesitate she went straight upstairs to change her dress and apron. She combed and redid her hair before placing a fresh *kapp* on her head, then returned downstairs. Just as she stepped into the kitchen Levi walked in the door.

Levi smiled and asked, "Are you ready to go?"

She smiled, *"Jah*, I am." She

took her coat and bonnet from *mamm*.

"*Danke mamm.*" *Levi* helped her into her coat and she put her bonnet on before they left. Once they were in the sleigh, Levi backed out of the driveway onto the road and headed toward town.

"I *lieb* to ride in the sleigh. She grinned. "It is so pretty when everything is all covered in pure white."

"*Jah*, it is." He smiled at her excitement. He *liebed* her so much and seeing her happy made him happy. He looked forward to the day he could make her his *fraa*.

The clip clop of Leo's hooves hitting the pavement was soothing, as they rode to the same restaurant where they had eaten supper the last time and went inside.

"Levi, Emily, it is *gut* to see

you again. Sadie, smiled, as she led them to a table and handed them menus. They both ordered the same special they had last time.

Levi looked over at Emily while they waited for their meal and said, "Emmy, *Ich lieb dich* with all *mie* heart and I hope it is not too soon, but I have to ask, will you marry me, be *mie fraa* and a *mamm* to Katie?" Levi waited anxiously for her answer. It would break his heart if she said nee, but as hard as it would be to accept, he would have no choice. He prayed that would not happen.

"Levi," Emily looked over at him. "*Ich lieb dich* too with *mie* whole heart and *jah*, I would *lieb* to be your *fraa* and *Boppli* Katie's *mamm*. She gave him a bright smile.

"That is *wunderbaar, Liewi*. You have made me a very happy *mann.*" He smiled just before they were interrupted by Sadie carrying both of their plates.

Once they were through eating they left and headed to see Bishop Yoder to see if they could be married this wedding season.

"Levi, I hope Bishop Yoder will have an open date and we can be married soon." Emily looked over at him.

"I hope he does too, *Liewi*. We are here, so we can go and talk with him." He smiled to try to reassure her. He stepped out and went around to help Emmy out of the sleigh. Since they would not be here long Levi wrapped his horse's reins around the post, put there for such times as this.

It was a little after four in the

afternoon when they walked up onto the porch together and Levi knocked. In just a minute the Bishop answered the door.

"*Guten tag,* Levi, Emily. Please *kume* in." Bishop Yoder smiled.

"*Danke,* Bishop Yoder. Levi motioned for Emily to step inside and he followed her in.

"Please have a seat, what can I help you with?"

Levi and Emily sat next to each other on the sofa and the Bishop sat in a chair across from them. A few minutes after they arrived Ruth the Bishop's wife, brought them a tray of home baked cookies, a cup of hot chocolate to Emily and *kaffi* to the Bishop and Levi. They thanked her and she went into the other room to give them some privacy, to talk with her husband.

"Now, what can I do for you?" He smiled taking a sip of his *kaffi.*

"Levi said, Bishop Yoder, we *lieb* each other and we would like to be married during this wedding season if we can." Levi smiled at Emmy.

"That is *gut* news and I am not surprised. Emily are you able to *lieb* and willing to raise Levi's *dochder* as your own?"

"*Jah*, I am. Bishop Yoder. I *lieb* Levi and Little Katie. I am blessed to be able to have them both in *mie* life."

"That is *gut*, I am glad to see that through prayer and with *Gott's* help, you have worked this out between you and you are going to be able to raise Little Katie together. She needs a *mamm* and a *daed*. I am happy for you both and you have *mie* blessing. Let me look to see what dates are available. I will be right back.

Levi smiled at Emmy just as the Bishop returned with a list of the few days available for their wedding date. After a few minutes they decided on Thursday December 8th. That would give them a chance to paint the inside of the *haus*. They thanked Bishop Yoder and headed out to the buggy. Levi helped Emmy onto the seat and went around to slide in next to her. "That went well." He smiled at her as he backed out onto the road to head to Emmy's *haus*.

"*Jah*, it did. I am so glad. I was a little nervous. It is so exciting, to now be able to plan our wedding." She grinned over at him. We need to ask our *newhockers* and I need to make *mie* dress." She grinned."

Levi, *liebed* to see Emmy so excited. He was as well. He was also very relieved she had agreed to marry him and they would soon be raising Katie together. He knew Emmy would make a *wunderbaar mamm* to his *boppli dochder,* soon to be hers as well, which delighted him."

"Levi, who do you plan to ask to be your *newhockers?* Emily asked, interrupting his thoughts.

"I figured I would ask the twins, Jacob and Joseph. Who are you going to ask to be yours?" Levi glanced over at her.

"Nancy and Rebekah since Brenda isn't old enough. I can hardly wait." She smiled.

"*Jah*, it will be nice to be together in our own home. I am looking forward to that." Levi pulled into Emily's driveway and parked in front of her back step. He went around, helped her out of the sleigh and walked her to her door. He leaned down and briefly placed a kiss against her soft lips, "*Guder nacht, Liewi. Ich lieb dich.* I will see you tomorrow."

"*Danke.* for supper and the nice sleigh ride Levi, *Ich lieb dich* too. "She smiled up at him before she went inside.

Chapter Twenty-One

Thanksgiving morning was dreary, it looked as if it could snow at anytime. Emily was glad the week was almost over. She had only seen Levi a few times since their sleigh ride and she was missing him. He worked during the day at the furniture store and in the evenings, he, his *daed* and *bruders* were painting the *haus*, which she really appreciated. Today would be different at *maami* and daadi's, thankfully they would be able to spend most of the day together. *Then* it was only a week until they would be married, she could hardly wait. She and her *schweschders* had helped *mamm redd* up the kitchen after breakfast. They were now helping the *buwes* load the dishes they were taking to *mammi and daadi's,* for their afternoon meal. *Emily* was glad they did not have too far to go.

When they arrived at *mammi* and *daadi's, daed helped mamm down and the buwes* helped the *maedels,* then took the buggy to the barn before *kuming* inside. As they walked through the door they could hear laughter. Emily her *mamm* and the *maedels* took the food to the kitchen and then went into the front room to greet everyone.

Levi walked up to her and said "Happy Thanksgiving, *Liebchen.* I have missed you this week." He smiled.

"Happy Thanksgiving, I have missed you too. Soon we will be together, I can hardly wait." She smiled back.

"*Jah,* I will be glad too, when we do not have to part each *nacht.*

Before Emily had a chance to say anything else, *mammi* said the meal was ready. They all took their seats around the tables that had been set up.

Levi and Emily sat down along with everyone else and

daadi bowed his head to silently pray over the meal. Once he was finished he started passing dishes around the table and everyone filled their plates. Soon they started visiting again. Levi was sitting next to Emily and he said, "We completed the painting. Our *haus* is ready for us to move into."

"That is *wunderbaar,* I can hardly wait to see it *now* that it is finished." Emily said excitedly.

"It will not be long now." He grinned.

The rest of the day pasted quickly and everyone had a *gut visit.* The *maedels* helped *redd* up the kitchen, while the *menner* folded and put the extra tables away.

When everything was done and they were all ready to go home, " Emily said, " I have enjoyed being with all of our *familye* today. We have a lot to be thankful for. I am tired, although I enjoyed it."

"*Jah* it has, but it was a *gut* day." Levi agreed.

She smiled and they walked out together. Levi helped her up into her *familye's* buggy and then walked over to ride home with his *familye*. Thankfully it had only snowed lightly, so the roads weren't too bad, but they expected it would snow again soon.

Chapter Twenty-Two

The Following Thursday when Emily woke up, she glanced over at her *schweschder*. "Good morning, Nancy. It's a beautiful morning, cold but clear. Thank the Lord. Can you believe it's finally my wedding day!" She grinned real big."I'm so glad it's here, but I'm so nervous."

"Good morning, Emily. I think most brides are nervous on their wedding day. I think that's pretty normal." Nancy gave her a hug.

"True. Well, the snow hasn't all melted, but at least it's enough that our guests should be able to get here for the service and ceremony and I'm so pleased to see the sun shining."

After making sure everyone was dressed in their *gut* clothes and a last-minute check to be sure Emily's blue dress, black *kapp*, and apron were all in order, *mamm* ushered the *familye* downstairs. She then resumed her place in the kitchen, making sure everything would be ready for the meal after the wedding ceremony, which would take place in their front room.

Emily hugged *mamm* before she and Nancy left the kitchen to find their place on the bench in the front row. Emily sat down on Levi's left. Nancy and Rebekah were seated to Emily's left, both dressed in light blue dresses to match hers. Levi looked quite handsome in his black coat, light blue shirt and black hat. His *bruders* Jacob and Joseph, were dressed the same as Levi. He didn't look the least bit nervous. Emily wished she could say the same for herself....she'd had butterflies in her stomach all morning. She prayed everything would go well.

As soon as the vows were exchanged, some of the women would head into the kitchen to act as servers, for the several hundred people who were expected to arrive that afternoon.

At nine o'clock Bishop Yoder, Minister Zook and Deacon Miller escorted Levi and Emily into another room. While they were being counseled on the duties of marriage, the congregation sang hymns.

When they returned, the Bishop began his sermon. He spoke on the marriages in the Bible and how *Gott* had brought the couples together. He told Levi and Emily that *Gott* had brought them together today to become one. It was close to noon by the time the sermon was concluded and Emily was very nervous by the time the Bishop asked her and Levi to step forward.

They held hands and smiled at each other. The Bishop placed his hands on top of theirs and prayed for a blessing over them. With the prayer finished, he addressed Levi and Emily. "Are you willing to enter together into marriage as *Gott* in the beginning ordained and commanded?"

"*Jah*," they both answered.

"Do you believe the person standing next to you is the mate *Gott* has chosen for you?"

Again they both said, "*Jah.*"

The Bishop read their vows and once Levi and Emily agreed to abide by them. He said, "You are now husband and wife, until the Lord separates you by death." He smiled.

Levi and Emily smiled at him and then at each other, as they took their seats at the *eck* table along with their *newhockers*. On each table sat a glass jar with stalks of celery inside for decoration along with *mamm's* best dishes. Beautiful cakes, bowls of candy and fruit filled every empty space. Emily glanced down at her plate filled with roast chicken, duck, mashed potatoes, dressing and creamed celery. It smelled *wunderbaar*. She took the first bite and said, *Ack* this is so *gut*."

"Are you okay?" Levi whispered next to her.

"*Jah*, I am now and I am starving." She smiled up at him.

He squeezed her hand gently. "I am too. This is the best day of *mie* life"

"Mine too." She smiled at him. "I'm so happy to be your *fraa*."

"You have made me the happiest *mann* in this community today," he said softly.

When they were through eating, their friends and family came by the table to visit with them and some of their friends gave gifts. The family would wait until they went to visit in the next few weeks to give their gifts.

By the time that the cake had been cut and served, the singing finished and the guests were leaving, Emily was exhausted. It had been a *wunderbaar* day, one of the best days of her life and one she would never forget, but she was glad it would soon be time to go their new *haus*.

"It's been a long day and I think it's time I took you home. Levi smiled at her.

"I need to stay and help *Mamm* finish up here first, Levi."

"*Ack*, Nee. I've done all I am going to do tonight," her *mamm* said. "Levi is right—you look exhausted, it is time you go home. You can *kume* back in the morning and we will finish the *redd-up* then."

Emily hugged her m*amm*. "Okay, we will be here in the morning for sure and certain."

"Before you go I have something for you." *Mamm* handed Emily a package.

"*Mamm* , you and *Daed* took care of the expense for the wedding and *mie* dress."

"*Jah*, but the *maedels and I* made this for you both. We wanted you to have this for your bed."

Emily gasped when she opened the box."*Ack*, it's a wedding ring quilt! Yellow, green, orange and rust on an ecru background....it's so beautiful. *Danki*, it will look *wunderbaar* on our bed." Emily hugged her *mamm, daed and schweschders.*

Levi nodded. "*Danki,* it will keep us warm, for sure and certain."

Before they left, Levi's parents Gideon and Faith handed Levi a card. "Emily you look so beautiful and we love you both so much. We wanted you to have this wedding gift from us and *the kenner.*"

Levi and Emily opened the card together and they gasped when Levi read out loud what was written inside. "We moved *Aenti* Elizabeth's bed out and replaced it with a new bed for you. *Mamm, daed,* and *kenner* Thank you so very much." They hugged *mamm* and *daed* and thanked the kenner.. "This is a very nice gift and we so appreciate it."

"You're welcome. We wish you much happiness, we *lieb* you both."

Levi's *mamm* and *schweschder's* offered to keep Katie tonight. After kissing the *boppli* goodnight and saying goodbye to their *familyes* and *frienden*, Levi helped Emily into the sleigh. He had decided to bring it, since it had been snowing again.

"This has been a *wunderbaar* day, but I am tired." She smiled.

"*Jah*, it has been and I am glad we are now married and never have to part, we can be together always." He smiled as he pulled into the driveway of their *haus*. He was looking forward to showing her the inside now that the painting had been completed."

Levi came around, lifted her down from the sleigh and carried her into the *haus.*

"*Ack*, Levi, our own *haus.*" Wonder brightened her eyes as she saw the new colors. "I *lieb* the kitchen. The light yellow is so *schee,* and this table. We will enjoy eating here together."

"*Jah*, we will and I look forward to us having our meals here together also." He smiled."

Emily's gaze moved around the place and her joy in knowing it was theirs reflected in her eyes. He was thankful he, *daed*, and the *buwes*, had taken the time to paint it.

"Levi, *Ich lieb* it and *danki* for it, my rocking chair and Lieben, our puppy, but this is too much." She stood and hugged him.

"*Nee* it isn't. One of my

greatest pleasures in life is being able to make you happy." He hugged her back and kissed the top of her head "

Levi followed Emily up the stairs, where he showed her the new painted walls in the four bedrooms for their future *kinner*. He then took her in to show her master bedroom which now held the new double bed, his parents and siblings had given them as a wedding present.

"*Ack*, Levi, these are *wunderbaar*. The colors of bedrooms and the bathroom are *schee*. When they walked into their bedroom she said, "Ack, I *lieb* our room and the new bed. It was so nice of your parents and siblings to get it for us."

Levi had to smile when color filled her cheeks, as she looked at their room and the new bed. "I am glad you like it."

"It's *wunderbaar!* I've never seen one more beautiful. Light oak is just what I would have chosen *mieself.* "She smiled at him.

"I am glad you are happy with it." He hugged her." I am going to fill the wood box and stoke up the fire. Why don't you get ready for bed? You are exhausted. I'm going to settle Leo and then I'll be up."

Chapter Twenty-Three

Emily spread the wedding ring quilt on the bed, then went into the bathroom to brush her teeth and took a nice warm bath. By the time Levi came upstairs, she had dressed in her night gown and was sitting against the headboard with her pillow propped behind her.

"I brought you a cup of hot
chocolate, I thought it might
relax you so you can rest
better."Levi handed her one of the
mugs he held and slid in next to
her with his own cup.

"*Danke*, it is *gut,*" she said,
after taking a sip of the warm
chocolate."

"*Welkom*, the quilt looks nice
on the bed."

Emily pulled it up over her and
admired it. I think it does too, *Ich
lieb it*." She smiled and continued
to sip her warm drink.

Levi leaned back against his
own pillow and sipped his cocoa.
When they were through, he
placed both of their empty cups on
his night table and drew Emily
into his arms. She thanked *Gott*
for allowing them to mend their
relationship, so they could and

have a future together.

The next morning Levi and Emily picked up Katie and went to Emily's parent's *haus*. They helped *redd* up and then stayed for an early supper with Emily's *familye,* before they headed home. After saying their goodbyes, they went back to their new *haus.* They decided due to the weather, to wait one more day before leaving on their two week trip, to visit *familye.*

When they got to the *haus,* Levi helped Emily inside with Katie. He added wood to the fire so it would stay warm. "I am going out to the barn to feed. I will not be gone long."

"Okay, I am tired. Now that Katie is settled in her cradle, the *buwes* brought over last night. I think I'll take a bath and relax."

Levi kissed her and headed out to the barn. He, Emmy and Katie would be gone for two weeks and his *bruders* would be doing all the chores, until he and Emily returned. He wanted to make sure he set out enough hay and oats tonight for them to feed. His *bruders* offered to take Lieben home with them, while he, Emily and Katie were gone. The pup was too small to stay home yet. A half hour later he came in, hung his hat and coat in the mudroom and checked on Lieben before heading upstairs. Emily was sitting up in bed and Levi slipped into his pajamas and slid under the blankets next her. "*Ich lieb dich, Leibchen.*

"*Ich lieb dich* too. This has been a nice day. I enjoyed visiting with *mie familye.*

"*Jah*, it has. Jacob really cares for Nancy. I hope everything works out for them."

"*Jah*, I do too. She cares very much for him as well. She told me he asked her to marry him next wedding season and she accepted. I know he will make her a *gut ehemann* and she will make him a *gut fraa.* We should pray about this and if it is *Gott's* will, it will be so." Emily smiled at her new *ehemann.*

"*Jah*, we will pray for them together." He smiled and kissed her forehead. "Now, it has been a *gut* two days but you look very tired"

"I am tired. It has been a *wunderbaar* two days. I enjoyed the wedding and spending time today with our *familyes,* but the best part is being here with you, *mie ehemann.*" She smiled and slid down into his arms.

"And me with you. You are *mie* life, Emily. I am so thankful *Gott* brought us together again, we are so blessed."

"*Jah,* we are." Emily kissed him. " I am thankful too, you are *mie* life as well, *Ich lieb dich* with *mie* whole heart."

"*Ich lieb dich* with *mie* whole heart as well, *Liewi.*" Levi said as he drew Emily into his arms and thanked *Gott* for allowing them to be together.

The following morning as they left their *haus,* Levi prayed they would have a safe trip to visit relatives and *Gott* would bring them back home safely. They went to the next District to Levi's

aenti and *onkels' haus* to spend
some time first. Then the next
couple of weeks went by quickly
as they spent their time visiting
relatives in other districts and
receiving several practical gifts as
well as clothes and blankets for
Katie. When it was time to leave,
Levi and Emily were sorry to say
goodbye, but ready to head home
and spend Christmas the next
morning with their *familyes*. When
they pulled up to their *farmhaus*
Levi said, "*Ich lieb dich mie fraa,*
shall we go inside our *haus*?"

"*Jah, mie ehemann,* I am ready
and *Ich lieb dich* too." Emily
smiled. I am looking forward to
spending Christmas with our
familye. Katie's first Christmas.
They looked down at their
precious *boppli* and realized she
was sound asleep. It had been a

long day for all of them and they were exhausted.

I am too, *Liewi* and we will enjoy her together as well.

Levi helped Emmy and Katie down from the sleigh and they walked into their *haus* glad to be home.

Epilogue

Emily climbed out of bed and smiled at Levi Christmas Morning. They had been in their new *haus* for two weeks now, but had only spent a couple of nights here before their trip. It had Christmas greenery in the windows and a line strung in the doorway for cards from family and friends Nancy, mamm, Brenda and Susan had added while they were gone so it would look festive when they returned and they both appreciated it. Christmas today and second Christmas tomorrow they would spend with their *familye's*.

"Merry Christmas, *mie ehemann*. I am looking forward to spending Christmas today and second Christmas tomorrow with you, Katie and our *familyes*." She grinned.

Levi drew Emily into his arms and kissed her. "Merry Christmas to you too, *mie fraa*. I am looking forward to spending it with you, Katie and our familyes too." He grinned down at her.

"As much as I would like to stay right here like this with you." She smiled up at him." I guess I better feed, and dress Katie, so we will be ready to go over to *mamm* and daed's, for breakfast."

"*Jah*, as much as I would like to as well. I am afraid you are correct. When I went out to feed earlier, I fed Lieben and let him out to run around, since he will be in his kennel while we are gone." Levi told her.

"*Danke,* I appreciate that." She smiled and kissed his cheek.

When they were ready, they picked up Katie, her packed diaper bag and their gifts for the family. They headed to *mamm & daed's* and when they arrived they placed the gifts on the table next to the window, by the Pine boughs and red, Christmas candles. They would be handed out tomorrow on second Christmas. They walked into the kitchen and sat at the table about the same time as the *menner.*

"*Ack gut* you are all here. We are ready to eat."Noah sat down to join them and said the silent prayer.

When Noah started the food bowls around the table Levi leaned over to Emily and said, "Merry Christmas again, Liebchen *"he* smiled.

"Merry Christmas to you too, Liewi." She said.

They all visited during the meal. It

was so nice that they would be able to gather here with both *familyes,* at Levi's parent's *haus* together to share Christmas. After breakfast and the kitchen was *redd* up, they all climbed into the sleigh and headed to the Graber *haus.* Levi's *mamm* met them at the door. After exchanging hugs and Christmas greetings, they went into the front room to join the others on the sofa and the *kinner,* all but the *boppli,* settled on the floor. They had just sat down when Nancy slipped in beside Emily. We have not had a chance to talk much since you moved. I am glad you are here, I have missed you.*"* She pretended to pout and Emily grinned at her.

"We wouldn't have missed it. We always enjoy Christmas with both of our *familye.* Our trip was *gut* we had a nice visit with everyone we do not see but once a year. We explained we would like to be home to be able to be ready to spend Christmas with both *familyes* here. They were all very gracious and understood. We enjoyed out trip but we are glad to be home."

"I am glad you are home too, for sure and certain." Nancy replied.

"Thank you," Emily smiled. "I'm glad to be able to be here with all of our *familyes too*."

Emily glanced across the room and noticed Levi looking her way. When their eyes met Levi smiled from where he was visiting with his twin *bruders* and a blush filled her cheeks as she smiled back at him.

In a few moments Noah, Levi's *daed* stood up and cleared his throat, he then sat down to read the Christmas story from the Bible in Luke chapter 2. He gave a little message afterwards, to give a good start to Christmas morning.

Emily *liebed* the Christmas Story and thought he gave a wonderful Christmas message, about how Jesus *liebed* us so much he came to this earth as a *boppli* and then died many years later as a sacrifice for our sins, rising again in three days. How He was in

Heaven now watching over us and if we believe in Him, when He returns, He will take us home to Heaven to live with Him for eternity.

Emily was so thankful, she knew Jesus. What a wonderful message to start the Christmas holiday with and as he finished his message, he smiled said, "Merry Christmas. Be safe, Love one another, be kind to one another and enjoy your *familyes* for the rest of the day."

Now that Noah had read the Christmas story, Faith, Ruth and the *maedels* served sandwiches and then cookies for desert. It was a light lunch day due to all the *familye* coming tomorrow for second Christmas, when they would serve a large sit down meal.

Once they had eaten they spent the rest of the day in front of the fireplace. They laughed, played board games and pieced puzzles together, then the *kinner* each opened a small gift from their parents.

That night upstairs, Emily told

Levi, "I don't know when I've ever had such a nice Christmas day."

"You're right, *Liebchen*. I don't know when we have either. There is so much *lieb* here. We enjoy just being together, laughing, sharing a meal and playing games, that is what makes the holiday special for us and we are so blessed to be a part of this *familye* and community. Even tomorrow, on second Christmas when we do share gifts, they will be useful, practical gifts, home made with thoughtfulness and love."

"*Jah* and as far as I'm concerned those are the best ones to receive." She smiled brightly.

"I couldn't agree more, L*iewi, Ich lieb dich.*" Levi turned out the light, he then drew Emily into his arms and kissed her. He *liebed* holding her. *Guder nacht*, I'll see you in the morning."

"*Ich lieb dich too, guder nacht.*

Second Christmas morning the sun peaked over the horizon just as Levi and Emily walked into the kitchen. It was cold and snow was still on the ground, but the sun was shining for which Emily was very grateful, It just seemed that when the sun was shining it brightened everyone's day. "*Ack,* someone has been busy," Emily said when she noticed the table had already been set. *Mamm* was placing the bowls of oatmeal on the table just as the *menner* joined them and took their seats. "I'm sorry we would have *kume* over sooner and helped if we had known you were starting early." Emily apologized.

"*Jah, Mamm* and we would have come downstairs earlier to help you too." Nancy apologized as Brenda and Susan nodded.

"*Ack, nee,* I wanted you *maedels* to sleep in some and now breakfast is ready."*Mamm* smiled at the *maedels* as they took their seats at the table.

"*Danke* that was very thoughtful *mamm*," Emily said and the others agreed and thanked her as well. Just then the *menner* came in from the barn and joined them at the table.

They had barely finished the *redd up*, when Levi's *familye* came in the door of the kitchen. They all greeted each other. Emily was so excited to spend hers, Levi's and Katie's first Christmas as a family together. Ruth had asked the second time she saw Emily, for her to call her *mamm* and she had been delighted to, so she had been *mamm* to Emily every since."

The rest of the *familye* piled in the door a few minutes later, with everyone talking and excited. The women stayed in the kitchen to help set the food out for the meal. Once it was all ready and on the large tables, the *familye* gathered around sitting together and then Everyone bowed their heads for the silent prayer.

After the noon meal the *familye* went into the front room and sat all around in front of the fire. They shared *kaffi* and cookies, visited and exchanged their gifts with one another. By late afternoon everyone was tired and decided to head home.

They had spent an enjoyable afternoon with all the *familye*.

Once they were settled upstairs in their bed, sitting up against their pillows. Emily said, I *liebed* everything I received today, but the most special was the Star flower quilt in yellow, red, royal blue and Kelly green on an ecru background, from your *familye,* It was so thoughtful of your *mamm* and *schweschders*, *Deborah* and Maryann, to make this for me and *Ich lieb* it.

This has just been a nice day ain't so?" Emily said. She leaned over and laid her head on Levi's shoulder, as they spent a few minutes together before going to sleep.

"*Jah,* it has been a very *gut* day for all of us. It is a *Shee* quilt for sure and certain. *Mamm* and the *maedels* have always *lieb* to quilt."

"*Jah*, it has. *Ich lieb* the Bonnet and gloves, from *mie mamm*, *daed*, and the *kinner. Also the* embroidered dish towels, pillowcases and handkerchief's from *Mammi* and *Daadi* Mast. The best part of *mie* day though was being with you and, Katie. I *lieb* the *shee* cedar chest you made for me, *danke* so much." She looked up at him with a bright smile.

" *Welkom. Danke*, for the *shee* new shirt and scarf you made for me." Levi kissed her softly. "I am glad you like the chest. It will be *gut* to store the quilts we received as gifts or if you make one you want to keep."

"*Jah*, you are right it will be *wunderbaar* for them. As you know, *Ich lieb* quilts." Emily grinned..

"*Jah* for sure and certain, you do. He grinned back and now you will have a choice of quilts you want to place on our marriage bed. The rest you can use the cedar chest to store." He smiled.

"*Ack* Levi, that makes me very happy! *Ich lieb* quilts. We now have six and they are all *wunderbaar!*" She grinned excitedly. I will enjoy teaching

Katie how to quilt when she is old enough.

He chuckled. "I am glad, I want you to be happy. Now as much I would *lieb* for us to stay right here talking together all night, you are very tired, it has been a busy week and Katie will be up wanting a bottle in a few hours, so you need to rest while you can." Levi smiled and kissed her forehead as they slid under the warm quilts so they could go to sleep. Before he dozed off though, he prayed, *Danke Gott, for me wunderbaar, fraa, dochder, familye and the enjoyable last couple of days as well as everything we have. Danke for loving us so much, that you sent your only Son, to die for us, to provide a way to salvation so we could accept him as our Lord and Savior and be able to one day live in Heaven with you for eternity. That is the most wunderbaar gift of all!*

Books by this Author

A Doctor For Abby
Doctor St. Nick
A Change of Heart
Dolls And Diamonds Book 1
A Doll For Heather Book 2
Joanna's Dollhouse Book 3
Loving Emily Book 1
Ellie's Amish Sweetheart Book 2
Sleigh Bells in the Snow
A Bundle of Secrets Book 1
A Hidden Secret Book 2
Violets For An Amish Girl
Peonies On An Amish Quilt
An Amish Family Blessing
Doctor Braxton's Kentucky Bride
A Christmas Miracle

Christmas In Amish Country
Book 1
Annie's Return to Amish Country
Book 2
Holly's Dilemma In Amish
Country Book 3
Christmas Belles of Georgia
Co-Authored with
  Rose Allen McCauley
  Jeri Odell
  Debra Ullrick
  Smoky Mountain Christmas
Co-Authored with
  Delia Latham
  Rose Allen McCauley
  Amber Stockton
  An Amish Christmas in Rocky
Comfort

Dear Reader

Thank you for reading this story. I hope you enjoyed this book set in an Amish Community in Missouri. If you enjoyed this book please go to www.amazon.com and leave a review. I would greatly appreciate it. ☺

Author Bio

Jeanie Smith Cash lives in the country in Southwest Missouri, in the heart of the Ozarks with her husband, Andy. They were high school sweethearts and have been blessed with a daughter, son, son-in-law, four grandsons, two granddaughters, two grandson-in-laws, two granddaughter-in-laws, one future granddaughter-in-law, eleven great-granddaughters and two great-grandsons. Jeanie feels very fortunate to have her family living close by. Jeanie and her family are members of New Site Baptist Church and attend regularly. When she's not writing, Jeanie loves to spend time with her family, spoil her grandchildren, read, watch the St. Louis Cardinals play baseball, collect Mickey & Minnie's, porcelain, & Raggedy Ann & Andy dolls, crochet, and travel. She is a member of American Christian Fiction Writers, she has twenty-one books published, and four short stories in magazines. She loves to read Christian romance, and believes a salvation message inside of a good story, could possibly touch someone who wouldn't be reached in any other way. Jeanie loves to hear

from her readers, so please feel free to contact her:
Email: jeaniesmithcash@yahoo.com
Facebook.com/jeaniesmithcash
Twitter.com/jeaniesmithcash

Thank you again for reading my book, I hope you enjoyed this story.
God Bless,
Jeanie Smith Cash

Made in the USA
Columbia, SC
11 February 2023